Wolf In Disguise Trilogy

An Erotic BBW Werewolf Pregnancy Romance Series

By: Jodie Sloan

Yap Kee Chong

8345 NW 66 ST #B7885

Miami, FL 33166

Createspace

Get Future New Releases In This Series For 99 Cents

http://eepurl.com/7jbHr

Like Us On Facebook

https://www.facebook.com/pages/JodieSloan/180879798753822

TABLE OF CONTENTS

Once Bitten

CHAPTER 1

"You really should be more careful, because you really seem like you have a lot on your mind these days. Could it have something to do with the fact that you're turning 30 in the next three days? I don't know why everybody gets caught up on numbers, because it really means nothing in the long run. We all know that we are getting older and then we start taking stock on our life and wondering if we have made the right choices or not. I for one don't believe in any of that and I live as if that day is going to be my last." Anne is Sal's best friend and they have known each other for over 10 years.

Sal looks at her friend and knows that most people would never understand their relationship. It wasn't like they were carbon copies of each other and just looking at Anne made her see just what kind of differences there were between them. They both had a healthy appetite for sex and the exploration of the flesh, but Anne was more outspoken and didn't mind walking up to a guy and placing her hand on his cock to get his attention.

"Anne, you know that I've been searching for that one for some time and there has only been one person that has come close and we both know who that is." Josh had been the one that got away, someone that had made her heart flutter and her body tingle with excitement every time he was around. It wasn't like Sal had anything to worry about, because her blond hair and dazzling blue eyes were more than enough to bring the boys around. That was the problem and most of them that she had met were still little boys trying to be a man, when Josh had been the exact opposite.

"You know, you just put salt into those cookies and I really don't think the children are going to like that." Sal was frustrated and grabbed the mixture and the bowl and threw both of them into the trash. Her hands were shaking and her mind was constantly running over the facts of last summer over and over again. "Don't get bent out of shape, we can make another batch and it won't take us more than a few minutes to get them into the oven. I came over here because you sounded frantic on the phone and I thought that I could help. I don't know why you just don't call him, or is it something to do with pride and the fact that he hasn't called you from the moment that he left here last summer?"

"I just don't get it, because we had a nice time and I'm using that term loosely, because what we did in the bedroom can only be described as euphoric. He did things to me that I didn't even know was possible, bringing me to the point of ecstasy over and over again until I couldn't move my limbs. His stamina was more than I could hope for and all he would do was smile and keep giving it to me. I think my screams could've been heard all the way through the apartment complex and a few of the tenants have given me wry smiles that made me blush two shades of red."

Baking powder and icing sugar were all over their clothes, but Anne was trying her very best to get her friends mind off of a certain someone. They had talked about it at length and there were even times that Anne was a little jealous of her friend and the connection that she made with Josh. She had only met him that one time, but there was something animalistic and raw in his demeanor that made her feel like she was naked and vulnerable in his presence. She'd never voiced these emotions before, because frankly he really wasn't her type to begin with.

"Men are puzzles wrapped up in a paradox and they think that we're hard to read. I've always thought that men only had one thing on their mind, but there have been times that I've seen them with a lot more substance than that." Anne was referring to a man that she had met on the Internet and they have been corresponding for some time.

"I know you've seen him, Anne and he would have to be the dictionary meaning of tall dark and handsome. He was the one that asked me out and I was hesitant, but his persistence paid off and we ended up having a night that would live in infamy. I still can't get over how many times he brought the woman out of me, making me arch my back and feel his fingers digging into my skin as he made the headboard slam into the wall repeatedly. I came so many times that I thought that I was going to pass out from sheer joy with my heart beating so fast that I thought it was going to come out of my chest." Josh was the type of man that she could never get out of her system and she wasn't even sure if she wanted to.

"Sal, life is full of little disappointments and I know how this man affected you. He doesn't deserve that kind of loyalty, because we both know that he left you after that night with no word or explanation whatsoever. All he would tell you was that he had to leave and I think that was a coward's way to get out of something that was intimate. From what you've told me, I would say that he has commitment issues and you shouldn't give this guy the satisfaction of making you doubt yourself. You've only been with one other guy since that happened and I think it's because he's gotten underneath your skin." Sal couldn't deny that her life could've been a whole lot better without Josh coming into it, because now she was measuring each man by his standard.

Her hands were busy with the cookies and now she slipped the pan into the oven and closed the door. She always found that she could lose herself in baking, but with her birthday looming, she could only think of one person and nothing more. She really did think that he would come calling at some later date, but that was 10 months ago under the hot July sun. There was just something about him and the way that he touched her that made her feel like she was special and not just some one night stand that he had found to relieve himself of some frustration.

Running her fingers through her hair, she came back with flour all over the place and she could smell the chocolate chips cooking quite nicely in the oven. If there's anything better than freshly baked cookies for her kindergarten class, she didn't know what it was.

"I've tried my best to get you back on the horse, but I see that it is a losing battle." Anne touched her nose ring, wondering how she was so irresponsible to let this happen on a drunken binge. It wasn't like she wasn't used to these types of things, because she had tattoos and even a piercing on her belly button and over her clit. It had made sex that much better and gave her a sensitivity that made her crawl up the wall anytime somebody even touched it. She had been trying for some time to get Sal to do the same thing, but so far she had been reluctant. "Josh is just another man that doesn't know a good thing when he sees it."

"I just thought that we were meant to be and he was the only one that I found that had the entire package. He was kind, gentle and forceful when he needed to be and had the kind of cock that would make a grown woman fall on her knees in worship."

The phone began to ring incessantly, making Sal sigh and then go over to answer it with a gruff sounding voice. "This better not be someone asking me if I like my long distance service." The voice that came back after a moment of silence stopped her cold and made her heart begin beating all over again.

CHAPTER 2

"Sal, I'm going to take the cookies out of the oven, because I don't want them to burn." Anne noticed that Sal had been gone quite some time and whoever had been on the phone had definitely gotten her attention." She looked up to see Sal standing at the doorway, leaning against the threshold with her hand on her heart, licking her lips and then glancing in her direction.

"I don't believe it and if I hadn't heard it with my own ears I would've thought that it was some kind of mirage. That was Josh and I know we just finished talking about him and then just like that he calls out of the blue." Anne was shocked by this new revelation and looked towards your friend to see if she was trying to tease her or make some kind of joke at her expense. She steps up to her friend, her 5 foot to frame dwarfed by Sal's 5'8, 135 lb body, with a nice pair of D cup breasts, all natural and wearing very little makeup.

Anne put her hand on Sal's shoulder to steady her, giving her the support and comfort that she needs to make her realize that the man of her dreams had just come out of the shadows after all of this time. "I know you have been talking about him for some time, but what makes him think that he can come back into your life and see you again after everything he has done. He should be ashamed, crawling on his hands and knees at your door begging for forgiveness. Calling you is just not enough and I hope you slammed the phone down on his ear." Anne knew from just looking at her that she didn't do that and the fact that she had been talking to him for over 5 minutes confirmed the fact that she wanted more than just some kind of apology.

"Anne, he told me that we had a lot to discuss and that he wanted to see me tomorrow tonight. He's in town for some kind of meeting and he wanted to touch base. At first I wanted to scream at him, but then I said that I thought it was a good idea. What the hell is wrong with me and what kind of hold does this man have on me that I can't see straight any time that he comes up in conversation. There is no denying that there is an attraction, but it's not just in what he looks like, but it's also with his sultry words and the way that he looks at me like he is undressing me with his eyes. I don't think it's a good idea that I should go and see him, because I know what's going to happen. Then again, I've wanted a repeat performance for some time and maybe now I will not only get that but some kind of explanation to explain his actions."

Anne knew that it was wrong for her to say anything disparaging about Josh, because her place was at Sal's side, no matter if she was making a mistake or not. "I know that I can't convince you otherwise, so I will bend to convention and ask you what you need from me. You know that you can lean on me and I will be there without judgment or condemnation. This is your life and I will not try to dictate the way that you live it, no matter how much I disagree with you seeing him again." They had been friends for too long to let a man get in between them.

"I really do appreciate that and I am a bit frazzled at the moment and will need you to help me find something to wear and help me with my makeup before the date." Anne couldn't say no and they began to pillage her closet, coming up with absolutely nothing. "

"I hope you know that you don't have to bow down to any man and you have everything going for you. I just want you to know that he doesn't deserve you and I think that you can do better. Believe me, I know that there will be no changing your mind, but I thought as a good friend that I should at least try." She was applying her makeup, making sure that she didn't look like some kind of whore or too demure, but in between the two. There was a fine line between looking like you were asking for it and looking like you were teasing him to the point of explosion. After she had applied the makeup, she looked at her best friend and saw the sexually adventurous woman that she had known all her life. Josh didn't stand a chance and he would be putty in her hand before the end of the night or maybe vice versa.

They said goodbye and Anne walked down the hall shaking her head in disbelief that Josh had really been on the phone. That man had turned her best friend into a basket case, wallowing in self-pity and wondering what was wrong with her and why he would leave in the middle of the night.

Josh had just landed a few hours ago and was contemplating his next course of action, when he got this urge to call the one person that had touched him in more ways than one. Across town at this very moment was the woman that had captured his heart, left him a shell of his former self and there hadn't been a day that went by that he didn't think about her.

Josh was that tall dark and handsome type with green eyes and a body that would make any man jealous and any woman want to be with him. There were several times that he could've succumbed to his baser instincts with one female or another, but Sal had ruined him for any other woman. They couldn't compare to the attraction and lust that he felt for Sal. He felt bad that he had to leave last summer, but he was on an enforced break and had found something that he wasn't expecting.

Standing at 6 feet tall, 225 pounds of solid muscle, he wore suits that complemented his statue, never one to keep a low profile and always the center of attention. This was no different and he was wearing a navy blue suit with a blood red tie and white shirt that made him look powerful and commanding at the same time.

He felt like a little boy lost in his own thoughts, as he picked up the phone several times and just couldn't bring himself to make that phone call. Finally, he made this growl of contention, slammed his hand down on the dresser in front of him, then picked up the phone with his fingers dialing and waiting for someone to answer on the other end.

He heard her voice and it made him go ice cold with panic, until finally he found the strength to say those words that had been haunting him all these months "Sal, I'm in town for some business and I was wondering if you would like to catch up. We have a lot to discuss, but I will understand perfectly if you don't want to see me." He waited on bated breath, hearing the line go dead and then hearing breathing on the other end. He thought for sure that she was going to lambaste him, scream at him with several expletives, but all she did was finally agree to meet him. They decided on the same Italian restaurant that they had met on their first date, because it had sentimental meaning to the both of them.

As he hung up, he began to think of her last summer and wondered if she had changed at all in that time. Was she the same woman that she had been, a fiery, take no prisoners kind of attitude or had his betrayal of her trust made her into something that he wouldn't recognize. There was really only one way to find out and now the die had been cast and there was no telling what was going to happen from this moment on.

Walking over to the balcony, he threw open the doors and let the wind cascade through his dark hair. He felt the hairs on his arms begin to rise and then he put his hands on the railing, while looking out at the city and imagining what it would be like to see her again. The first time was unexpected, something that he wasn't prepared for and he had fallen into the trap that he had swore that he would never find himself in.

CHAPTER 3

Time stood still as he looked out at the city, not really seeing anything and his thoughts slowly drifting to the past. That summer, he had been in town because he was asked to stay away, until a decision had been made about his future.

He had no desire to let others decide his punishment, but the rules were there for a reason and he had broken several of them in the name of loyalty.

When he arrived in this town, he felt alone and drifting aimlessly, until he bumped into this woman. He was too distracted about what he was going through to watch what he was doing and he literally fell head over heels for this woman in red. She was tastefully dressed with a red dress with a white belt around her waist. It was short, but not too short, although he had to admit that her expanse of naked thigh was more than enough to ignite his libido.

"Watch where you're going...you fucking idiot." This woman was not very cordial, a little abrasive around the edges, but there was something in her eyes that made him reach out and take her hand. Once he did that, all of her protests had come to an end and soon they were standing and saying absolutely nothing to each other.

"I'm so sorry, and I guess that I was distracted. I hope I didn't hurt you." He was dusting her off and he could feel this electricity between them that couldn't be denied.

"I guess no harm was done." His fingers lingered a little longer than necessary on her clothing and he could feel the swell of her breasts and the smoothness of her skin on the pads of his fingers. There was a problem brewing down below his waist and he tried to think of anything to bring it under control, but it was of no use. It wasn't lost on him that she was looking in that direction and the way that she was biting her bottom lip was so endearing that he just couldn't let this moment pass without at least trying to get to know her better.

His hand had hers and she was swaying back and forth on her feet, her eyes dancing with her mouth slightly parted. "I don't usually do this, but could I possibly buy you dinner? I think it is the least that I can do, considering that I did knock you down and ripped that dress." The rip in question had given him that brief peak at her inner thigh and he wanted nothing more than to follow it with his tongue up to the moist center of her loveliness. "I'm not some kind of weirdo and I only want to pay it forward. I'm sure that the restaurant that I have in mind will meet your expectations, but you will have to dress up for the occasion." For some reason, he still had her hand and then he instinctively dipped his head and gave it a soft kiss.

"Okay, I don't see any reason why we can't have dinner together. Just don't get any ideas, because I carry mace and a taser in my purse. If you try anything fresh, I will be forced to use it." He wasn't usually attracted to women of this kind of attitude and backbone, but on her it worked.

They had dinner and then he suggested a movie and before long they were kissing and making out like a couple of love stick teenagers. To this day, he still doesn't remember what the movie was, because they really didn't get a chance to watch any of it.

Sal didn't sleep all that well, because she had vivid images of that night running around in her head. When she awoke, she still felt ill at ease about the meeting, but she had to get to her kindergarten class with the cookies that she had baked with Anne last night.

"Um, did you get dressed in the dark this morning?" Anne could see that the telephone call with Josh had really rattled her and she was wearing one red shoe and one black slipper, not to mention she seemed like she hadn't slept in ages. "That man has you wrapped up in knots, but I guess I might be just a little bit jealous. That being said, I think that we should go shopping and find you a dress that is going to knock his socks off and make his eyes come out of his head. It's the least that he deserves and you should make it appear that you have been living your life and not thinking about him at all."

The kids were bowled over by the cookies and they had their own names stenciled on the top in icing. Sal got lost in their youthful exuberance, watching them as they enjoyed each individual bite, until they were finished with this smile of jubilant glee on their faces. Instead of sugar, she had used a non-sugar substitute that wasn't going to make them so hyper during the afternoon. She was casually dressed in a black blouse and tight blue jeans.

They did go out and find this little black dress that didn't leave all that much to the imagination. At first, Sal was a bit hesitant to put it on, but with some gentle coaxing from her best friend Anne, she did. It did indeed hug her curves in all the right places and was short enough on the bottom that it gave a brief hint of more to come, as well as showed off her other more prominent assets. "I can't wear this."

"Sal, you are going to wear it and you are going to wear it without underwear." She looked at her friend in shock, but she learned a long time ago that Anne was not one to back down. She would do as requested, but mostly because it was naughty and gave her a feeling of vulnerability.

Twirling around, the dress moved with her frame and showed off her hard naked globes. They were the byproduct of several hours doing Pilates and jogging in the neighborhood. She knew that men in general couldn't walk by her without taking a second glance and even though she didn't feel that she was that sexy, she knew that men and some women had found her to be more than just that. The one thing that she hadn't done before was to cross the line with Anne, even though they did kiss when she was too drunk to care about anything at the Christmas party. They didn't do much more than that, necking a little but not taking it too far to ruin a friendship that had stood up to the test of time.

"That man is so fucked and he doesn't even know it." Sal had to smile, looking in the mirror and knowing that her friend was right on the money. "That will teach him that it's not right to run off in the middle of the night." Sal really wasn't listening and was only imagining what Josh's head would look like underneath the dress and how his tongue would slither in between her folds and make her feel that she was the only woman in the world. "I know that look and right now you are thinking about having sex with him. Try not to go too fast, because we all know what happened the last time you tried that with him." They bought the dress, but she didn't wear it out, because it would have caused an accident or two with those that were driving on the street becoming distracted and running their vehicle up a telephone pole.

Sal couldn't believe that she had bought such a garment, because it was a little bit more risqué than she was used to. It did make her feel more confident and secure in meeting with him, because now she would project the type of woman that she wanted to be. Just touching the fabric made her feel like a wanton slut and she had to swallow with the fear that it was too much. She came to the conclusion that she didn't care and that she was going to wear it despite herself. Every man would see her and begin to wonder what she looked like without it on and she had no doubt that she would feel exposed, but in a good way.

CHAPTER 4

Sal and Josh saw each other for the first time in 10 months and both of them are too tongue tied to say anything at all for the first few seconds. They stand at the precipice of going into the Italian restaurant, him looking at her and her looking at him in the same way that they had looked at each other all those months ago.

Sal wants nothing more than to tear his clothes off in the middle of the street, push him onto one of these cars parked nearby and ride him like a bucking bronco all the way to the finish line.

Josh imagines himself ripping at her clothes, stripping away her inhibitions and pushing up against her with her hands up against the wall.

They both shook themselves from their respective fantasies, him showing the obvious arousal of his affection pressed up against the fabric of his pants and her feeling a slight moisture that was now starting to drip down her leg. "I guess we should get a table and then order a bottle of wine." She liked Josh's suggestion and she followed him into the restaurant with her eyes burning a hole in his backside. He looked as good as ever, if not more so and she desperately wanted to touch him and feel him and then drive her teeth into his ass.

Josh could feel that she was sexually excited and could feel her eyes on him the entire time that he traveled the distance to their table. Opening up her chair, the squeaking of the wood against the floor was followed by her sliding into position and smoothing down her dress in order to keep things in place. She saw the flex of his organ and knew that she was getting to him.

"I'm not sure why I'm here and the way that we left it last time made me think that you would never be darkening my door again." She couldn't help but to stare at him over the table, watching as he drank from his glass of water and then taking an ice cube out and moving it back and forth across his neck. He didn't mean to try to excite her or turn her on, but he was feeling the heat and it wasn't because of the temperature outside.

"I know what I did was reprehensible, but you need to know that I have never stopped thinking about you." The plunging neckline of the dress gave him an unobstructed view of her cleavage and the slight droplets of sweat that were forming between them. The candlelight on the table was a nice touch and gave a nice romantic atmosphere that had them both moving around in their seat uncomfortably. "When I found myself back this way, I needed to get in touch with you and make things right. You have to know that it had nothing to do with you and it was something that I was going through that was more personal than anything else. I can't go into details, but I promise that I really didn't want to leave you."

His confession caught her by surprise, making her instinctively reach across the table and touch him in a soothing manner on the back of his hand. This slight physical contact lit the fuse between them and they were now aching for more than just the calamari in cream sauce. Their hunger was no longer for food, but was more for each other. "I don't mind telling you that I was hurt and I would like to say that I found somebody else. I can't do that and I came here with the express purpose of telling you that I'd moved on. Just sitting here looking at you and I know that that's not true and I feel so stupid to let you get underneath my skin like that."

"It's not one sided, Sal and I've wanted to return to your side from the moment that I left you. It just wasn't the right time and I was in no state of mind to give you what you needed. To be honest, I still don't know if I am able to give you what you need."

Sal had now moved her spiked black heels over to the other side of the table and was now rubbing her foot up and down his leg in a not so subtle way. She couldn't help it and there was no way that she could deny herself one more chance to touch him and feel him in the Biblical sense.

They finished their meal, but had no room for dessert and really didn't want to get too full for what they both had in mind. "I think that we should take a walk down by the beach." He nodded his head in affirmation, as they both left the restaurant and moved towards the beach where they could both hear the surf pounding against the shore. The sound of the water was soothing and the feel of the sand on their bare feet, as they took off their shoes was more than enough to make them want each other in more ways than one.

Josh had his hand around her waist and he could feel this overwhelming desire to kiss her, but he didn't want to make any unwanted movements that might spook her. He needn't have worried, because Sal was waiting for him to make a move and then she decided to make it for him. Turning in his arms, she raised herself on her toes, wrapped her hands around his neck and pulled him down for a kiss.

It was like coming home and they both sank into it until they were falling onto the sand each other's arms. They rolled around and let their fingers do the walking, but only touching and feeling with his hand up on her inner thigh, so close to her treasure trove that she was almost screaming out for him to go further.

"I've never met anybody like you, Sal and you have had me wrapped around your little finger from the moment that we met. I can't explain it, only that I felt this instant connection that went beyond just the physical, although the physical was there and I don't think I have to tell you that." She was now biting his neck and pulling on his earlobe with her teeth, squeezing his ass and getting a good feel for something that she had been missing all these months.

A police officer interrupted their fun and they scrambled to their feet, grabbing their shoes and laughing like crazy as they ran back to the restaurant. Sal's apartment was not too far away and they make it to the door before they were kissing once again. This time it was him kissing her, holding her tightly and never wanting to let her go. He was this close to invoking his animal instincts, but he had to pull himself away from the abyss before he did anything that he regretted.

Once they were inside, he looked around and saw that it was exactly as he remembered it and the only thing that had changed was instead of a black duvet on her king size bed, there is was a white duvet and billowing white curtains to go along with the motif. The window was open and she used her hand to push him onto the bed, until she was straddling his waist with her knees on either side of his body.

She could feel his appendage and started to go for his zipper, when she feels him pull away and it brings back that dejection that she had felt after that first night.

"I can't do this, unless you know the truth once and for all. Before I begin, I don't want you to say anything and just let me get it out before I lose my nerve."

"Oh my god...what is it...are you gay, married or some kind of sick cross dresser?" She felt his finger touch her lips, silencing anything else she had to say, and making her look at him with concern and wanting some kind of explanation.

He got up and started to pace back and forth, wringing his hands and mumbling something underneath his breath that she couldn't understand. "I wanted to tell you this that night, but I just didn't have it in me. We can't go any further until I get this off my chest, but I think you'll understand when you hear the words. You see, I am not exactly like most men and I am older than I appear. I've been around a very long time and I've seen it and done it all, but the one thing that I haven't done is fall in love. You gave me that opportunity and now you need to know that I am... I am a werewolf." It felt like a weight had been lifted off his shoulders, but when he looked at Sal, he saw nothing but a blank stare.

Suddenly, she began to laugh, pounding her fist on the mattress and then stepping up to him with a slap across the face that stung like nothing before. “Why you insist on giving me this story is beyond me. How did you think this was going to go? Did you really think that I would believe something like this? I want you to leave and this time I don’t want you to come...mmmpphhhhh.”

He kissed her, letting that passion ignite the beast within, until he was turning away from her and then glancing back in her direction with hair spreading all over his face and these angry looking fangs coming out of his mouth.

CHAPTER 5

Josh is a 116 year old werewolf that has seen everything and it all started on that fateful day back in the 1800s when slavery was still very much alive in the south.

He was the son of a prominent businessman and it wasn't unusual to have several young women and men at their beck and call. The slaves were brought together for a festival with food and drink from two plantations in the area. Josh wasn't supposed to be a part of it, as his father had to go out of town and that was when they had decided to have the party in his absence. It was a well-known fact that his father was ruthless and domineering and he didn't mind using the switch from time to time to keep his people in line.

The slaves on the other hand knew that Josh was different than his father, more caring and compassionate about their plight and found him to be somebody that they could trust.

"You have to come, Josh, because it's because of you that we are able to do this and enjoy a moment of freedom. Believe me, it takes a lot of courage for you to do this and I think that you should be a part of it. Nobody would look twice at you and I'll make sure that they know that you were responsible for all of this." Mason was one of the older gentlemen in the plantation, somebody in his early fifties, but still quite the work horse. He was used to hard work and didn't mind getting his hands dirty, but then again it wasn't like he had any choice. He'd often thought that maybe he could run away and find that Underground Railroad that people had been talking about, but that was for the younger generation.

Josh was looking out the window, his hands behind his back and a regal bearing showing through. His hair was long and in a ponytail, something that his father had strictly forbid him to do. He had done it to rebel against his father and he was always trying to get him into the family business, but he had no interest in slavery. He wanted them to be free, because the color of their skin shouldn't matter about their statue in life. He was of the impression that he could make a difference, but so far his interference had only caused strife between his father and those that he considered his employees.

"Mason, you know that I would love to join you and your people, but some way or another it would get back to my father and then all hell would break loose. I just don't think it's a good idea." Mason was not easily deterred and still pestered him until he finally agreed to make an appearance.

He walked into the party and the music came to a dead stop and everybody in the area stared at him like he was some kind of interloper. "I'm sorry and if you want me to leave I will do so." Nobody made a move towards him and then the music started up all over again and people began to dance around and enjoy themselves. He took it upon himself to serve them their food and drink, taking on the role that they usually did for him over the years. It was during that party that he met Isabella, a young African American woman with heaving bosoms, who was dancing around like she was already free. Her love for life and the way that she moved mesmerized him and had him staring at her like he couldn't believe that she was really there. The white dress was the perfect contrast to her ebony skin and he found himself moving towards her, not quite knowing what he was doing until they were moving together with their hands on each other's hips.

"I know who you are and my name is Isabella." With a touch of her fingers on his cheek, he found himself being dragged away from the party and over behind a nearby shed. The heat between them was palpable and he could see that she was sweating, giving off this sheen that made her even more desirable than she was before. Pushing him up against the shed, she began to undo his shirt, exposing his manly chest to her gaze. "You have a fantastic body and I have been watching you for some time from across the field. All of us know that you are trying your best to make our lives better and I think that I want to reward you with a gift for all your hard work and determination to change things."

Josh felt her hands begin to undo his pants, pulling his brown slacks over his finely toned ass, until she was taking him into her mouth and making him look over her shoulder at the countryside, still not believing that this was really happening to him. He was a hair trigger, especially being that he was only 19 years old at the time, cumming deeply into her throat and making her swallow it all.

She didn't give up there and continued to move her tongue in such a way that had him raging with new vigor. This time, he didn't shy away, lifting her until her dress was around his waist and her beautiful young flower was fluttering open to receive him. They looked at each other with eyes wide open, as he buried himself all the way to the base.

"AHHHHHHH." She cried out and wrapped her hands around his neck, holding on as he bounced her up and down on his lap. It was not the lovemaking of somebody that was in love, but more out of control and into a frenzy of sexual heat that couldn't be satiated without both of their bodies coming together. There were no words, only moans of arousal and excitement permeating the air, as he felt her lips caress his shaft and pull at him, as she came so hard that he couldn't help but to unload the burden within his balls.

They stayed joined, kissing and making out like they had known each other all their lives and then Isabella got carried away and bit him.

Josh felt her teeth and it only made him shoot one more spurt into her loins, making him sigh with contentment and look at her as she stepped away from him with a horrified expression on her face. "I'm so sorry and I hope that one day you will forgive me." She dashed off, glancing back one more time at the man that she had just sent into his own personal hell.

Josh stood there and felt strange, the night sky showing the first hint of the full moon and then he changed.

In the morning, he awoke to find that he had killed every living slave on the plantation. Mason was strewn over a picnic table with his throat ripped out and the rest of them were lying there with surprised expressions, as if they couldn't believe that their death had come from the hands of somebody that they trusted.

He tried to hide the bodies, burying them deep in the fields where they would never be found. His father was suspicious and thought that he had helped them escape, leading to him being locked up in the basement, until he felt the change come over him 30 days later.

When he awoke this time, he saw that he had killed his father, his blood still dripping from his fingertips and off of his chin. Pieces of his flesh still lie on the table, where he had consumed the meal and once again he tried to hide it by burying his body.

Over the course of three months, more bodies began to appear in town, but the wolf inside him had left them on the doorstep of the courthouse for everybody to see. He couldn't hide what he had done and eventually they would come to realize that he was responsible.

Josh knew that he couldn't stay there any longer and began to search out a cure for what Isabella had done to him.

He traveled the continents, going from one country to the next looking for any kind of help, while at the same time leaving a trail of bodies that followed him like the plague. He eventually resigned himself to his fate, but the death toll was too much for him to take and he started to experiment with animal blood. It wasn't as clean or intoxicating, but it did give him what he needed to curb the hunger when he turned on the full moon. That fateful day when he had changed would forever haunt him.

Chapter 6

"Now you know my whole story and you have seen me change with your own eyes." It took a lot of will power for him to show Sal a brief window into what he was. The concentration was more than he could take and he changed back so quickly that it was almost too fast. "I know that this is a lot to take in and you might need time to adjust. I just need you to know that you were the only one that I've ever come close to. Any time that I found myself falling for a woman in any regard, I would walk away before I did anything that would make her hate me for the rest of my life. I hid myself from them, but I thought it was high time that I share that part of myself with someone."

Sal didn't know what to think, but she couldn't deny what she had seen. "I think I would rather you have said that you were married, because I think that would've been a lot more easier to wrap my mind around. To be honest, I'm a little terrified that you are going to kill me like you did when you first changed all those years ago. Why would you think that it was any different with me and how are you going to stop your wolf side from killing me on the full moon?" These were words that Sal couldn't believe that she was actually uttering, but she was immensely curious about his life. It had to be lonely never able to love and she felt like she had to reach out to him in some way.

"I would never hurt you and there was something different about you that makes me think that there might be a future here. Can I be certain that I won't kill you on the full moon...no, but I feel that I can keep that part of myself in control. I've learned to embrace the wolf and I no longer lose myself when I change. In fact, I am two parts of a whole and it took some very unique meditation exercises from an old Chinese man to show me that I was capable of being both the wolf and the man. I still need to hunt, but that is my cross to bear and not yours. I hope you don't hate me for telling you this, but I would understand that you couldn't handle something like this."

Josh sat down on the bed, his legs dangling over the side and his heart breaking, thinking that Sal would be too traumatized to want to continue this relationship. "Josh, you have to admit that you've given me a lot to think about. I will say that I am not one to shy away from somebody's differences.

"Let me show you that I can be with you and not hurt you. The only way this is going to work is if you truly trust me and that you know deep in your heart that I would never harm a hair on your head." He took her hand and placed it against his heart, letting her see that he was still a man and then he kissed her gently.

Despite herself, she felt immediately attracted to Josh and this feeling had not changed since his confession a few minutes ago. The kiss was one sided and then it wasn't, as they made out and began to take each other's clothes off one item at a time. With each piece of exposed skin, Josh would kiss it lightly, leaving her feeling this buildup of sexual electricity that was causing her to want to see what he was hiding underneath his pants.

"I should have my head examined, but I just can't say no to you, Josh." He helped her with rising up and standing so that she could pull his pants and underwear down. His cock snapped against his stomach, as she reached out and grabbed it and pulled it towards her mouth. "Damn you for coming back into my life." With that, she sucked the head, tasting the fruits of her labor on the tip and then moving her lips down until nothing remained. She could feel his hands running through her hair and then pulling it in such a way that she was able to look up at him with her mouth full to see the satisfaction on his face.

"I've missed you more than you can ever know, Sal. Your lips feel like silk and your tongue seems to have a mind of its own." He closed his eyes, but it didn't remain so, because he wanted to see what she was doing. His mouth was open and he was still surprised by how easily she could play his body like a musical instrument. The tune that she was strumming was causing his body to react and before long he was letting go with a burst of love that she easily took.

His explosion had taken her back to that night that they had let their passions rule over their head. The way that he had attacked her that night was like an animal and she could still feel the friction of his thighs, as he pounded her into the bed with relentlessly fury. She had never been taken like that in her life and all she could do was climax several times over and lie back in a post orgasmic stupor afterwards. The way that he had given it to her was forceful and this time was more gentle and loving.

Slowly, she spread her legs and put them over his shoulders, letting him enter her with one long continuous thrust that took both of their breath away "YESSS...Oh god...what have I gotten myself into...OHHH...OHHH...OHHHH." His strokes were slow, but his cock demanded more than that and soon he began to move with an earnest that had that very headboard that he had seen last summer, slam up against the wall so hard that one of the picture frames fell to the ground with a horrible crash.

He turned her quickly, seeing her on her hands and knees with her head placed on a pillow and her eyes urging him on. He grabbed hold of her hips, spreading her wide and seeing the pink of his desired target waiting for him. He couldn't do anything, only looking at those raw and blood red lips, swollen and calling to him like some kind of siren of the sea. Bracing his feet on the mattress, he plowed forward with his hips, bringing to bear the full weight of his body up against her.

She could barely believe that she was now with the man that she had been thinking about all this time. His body, his words and the way that he held himself was too much of a temptation to pass up. It didn't matter that he was a wolf underneath his skin, because the one thing that she couldn't control was the all-encompassing love that she felt for him. "I love YOUUUUUUUU." She felt her body tremble and her insides begin to quake, squeezing and convulsing around his man meat. She could feel his cock swelling to mammoth proportions, the head about to let go with a volcanic white hot substance that would keep her coming back for more.

Josh tried to follow through with her orgasm, but it felt like she was trying to milk him of the very seed that he had been trying to hold onto. His breathing was getting shallow and he could feel that his balls were overflowing to the point of having nowhere else to go but to travel up the expanse of flesh of his length. He tried to think of anything to abstain from doing that, because he was feeding off of her pleasure and wanted to keep this going for as long as possible. Unfortunately, being apart for almost a year had taken its toll and he had no choice but to bury himself deep and give in to the sensation that was growing by the minute. This was by far stronger than anything that he had felt before and probably would ever feel again.

He felt her slapping at his chest, leaving behind red marks and he had his hands underneath her, as he felt the burning need to let loose coming upon him. “I'm...I'm CUMMMMMING.” His body betrayed him and it had only taken 20 minutes to hit the right buttons. Their clothes were discarded on the floor and across the bed and Josh lay down and put his head between her breasts, enjoying the softness of her body and listening to her heartbeat. They fell asleep, each one too exhausted or too overwhelmed by the emotional impact of what they did to keep their eyes open any longer.

As he drifted off to sleep, he began to have his doubts about whether they could be together. He thought that maybe what he had done to her last summer had broken her into a shattered doll.

What he didn't realize was that Sal was stronger than he gave her credit for. He had no idea that underneath it all she was capable of so much love and compassion and that just maybe there was room in her heart for somebody like him. They fell asleep in each other's arms, spooning with his hands around her and her head against his chest.

CHAPTER 7

The night was restless for the both of them even though they had just consummated their relationship with a wild night of lovemaking, but it didn't mean that their problems were over. In fact, she felt more confused than ever, waking at various intervals in the evening to look at him and know that what he had said about himself was true. She thought that it was all a dream, but it was too vivid and clear to be anything but reality.

She awoke around 5:00 AM in the morning, just as the sounds of nature were announcing a new day. At first, she didn't realize that Josh was with her, until she saw the lump under the covers and began to replay the evening over and over in her mind. She didn't realize it, but she had given her heart freely to a man that had left her last summer.

As she thought of what she would've done differently, she began to see that life would have been more confusing if he had stayed and maybe they both needed this time to get ready for the possibility of a real relationship. This curse had followed him, haunted him and gave him a moment pause when it came to falling in love. She had to give him credit for keeping this secret to himself, even though it was eating him up inside every single day. The hurt and pain of being alone was his weight to carry on his shoulders and she touched his chest and ran her finger down until she had met the V leading to the promised land.

It appeared that he was sensitive in that region, because he squirmed slightly and moved until he was flat on his back. The sheets had fallen away from his frame and was now giving her an unobstructed view of his body. The only thing that was covered was his manhood and all she had to do was lift the sheet slightly to see it lying against his thigh.

Touching it, she watched as it started to unfurl and she bit her lip wondering if maybe she could wake him up in a pleasant way. Not thinking about it, she tossed the sheets away from both of their bodies, as she moved into position and pushed his legs open to receive her. He was still sleeping, but she could see this smirk of pleasure creasing his features.

Her tongue attentively came out and touched his member, tasting a combination of both of their juices that was still there after what they did. She put her concentration on awakening his other senses, running her fingernails down over his chest and touching his nipples. She was breathing hot air across the head and then she leaned forward and sucked the knob into her mouth.

It began to grow under its own power, until it was surging with new energy and vitality. "I don't know what I deserved to be woken up like this, but whatever it is, please tell me and I will do it again." She glanced up and saw that he was lying against the pillow, his hands over his head and looking down at her with an appreciative grin. "I can honestly say that I've never been woken up in such a way and I'm glad that you were my first." It was almost like taking his virginity, but in an entirely different way altogether.

"Just relax, Josh and let me finish my breakfast in peace. I just need some cream for my coffee and I thought that you had more than enough to give me a little." She was teasing him, but then she returned to what she was doing, slamming her head down into his lap with his cock head pressed obscenely into her throat. She already knew that she was in love with him and that there was nothing that he could say, regardless if he was a werewolf or not that was going to stop her from claiming him as hers.

"By all means, get as much cream as you can and then we're going to have to have some kind discussion about where this is...OHHHH...watch the teeth." Sal had stopped his train of thought by grazing her teeth along the length of the shaft, biting lightly on the head and leaving behind indentations of bite marks. She thought that since he was some kind of wild beast underneath this tame exterior, then she should be something of the same in her own way. "You don't take any prisoners and I think I like that about you. I think that you would've made a great werewolf. You have the animal instincts and desire that would be needed for the hunt."

She was sucking his cock, but inside her own mind, she was thinking about what he said. She had never thought of it before, but maybe a life of being a werewolf one day a month wouldn't be so bad. She would have the strength and agility of more than just a human being and would be connected to him in a way that she could never be with anybody else.

She was distracted by his cock, as it was showing signs of excitement and more and more of his sauce was now spilling forth onto her tongue. It was perfect and gave her a new feel for the man, as he was squirming and thrashing his head back and forth on the pillows. His hands were bunched into the sheets and he was pulling at them and trying to keep himself from bursting.

"Sal, I'm going to give you fair warning and if you don't stop soon, then I won't be responsible for what happens next." Sal had no intention of stopping anything and was now moving her hands down his inner thighs and causing Goosebumps to pop up all over his skin. "Damn, you really want it that bad and who am I to argue with you." She had him in the palm of her hand and didn't want him to soon forget that she had this kind of power over him. With her mouth constantly moving and her tongue sliding around the head on each stroke back up, it was no wonder that she could feel the swell of his organ and the throbbing of his veins as he readied himself for the explosion to come.

This time, she wasn't going to miss a beat and she pulled him out at the precipice of him going over the edge. The palm sized mushroom began to pop with its own pulse and Sal had her mouth wide open with that tongue extended waiting for the inevitable.

The first shot went across her tongue and into her throat before she even had a chance to enjoy the flavor. The next few blasts pooled on her tongue and she let it linger there until he was finished, before showing him the result with her mouth wide open and then swallowing it without a second thought.

Crawling up until she was in his arms again, Sal placed her head against his shoulder and watched as his chest began that steady rise and fall with each breath. "I hope you know what you're doing, Sal. Last night and this morning has only convinced me that we could be more than just passing ships in the night. I just need to know if you can accept me for who I am, because there really is no way of changing me. I've tried too many times and I think I've lost count on how many rejections has happened over the years. I'm sure that there is a cure, but everything I've tried thus far has been in vain. You don't know how many times I've cried myself to sleep thinking that there was no hope and that I was doomed to this curse for the rest of my life."

"I know that it had to be hard living in the shadows and never able to tell anybody what you were."

"Sal, I think for once in my life that I've begun to see that there is one person that can accept me. I thought for sure when I told you what I was that you would run screaming into the night and I wouldn't have blamed you one bit. It was a surprise to see that you were so ready to live with a man that becomes a beast once a month."

"Josh, in the grand scheme of things what is one day a month? I mean, everybody has their baggage and you just so happened that have a wild and uncontrollable animal inside of you. We all have that, but you have taken that to a whole different meaning. If I was going to be perfectly honest, I will say that I was taken aback by your confession and even more so when you changed so abruptly."

"Sal, that wasn't my true form and that was only a brief peak of what I will become in the next few days. If you want, I can disappear during that time and I won't hold it against you." Sal touched his chest and ran circles around his nipples, seeing him arch his chest and sigh with contentment.

"If I am going to be involved in this, then I should be all the way in." They embraced and this new budding relationship had now taken form.

Secretly, Sal began to wonder if maybe he would think that this was too much for her and leave her in the middle of the night like he had done before. This was the fear that she was now going to have to live with, even though she suspected that he would never put her through that kind of pain again.

Josh on the other hand felt that there was a possibility for them, but he wasn't getting his hopes up by any means. He knows that this is a hard thing for her to understand and even though she says that she wants to make him a part of her life, he still doesn't know if she believes it or will follow through.

"I'm glad that you said that, but I wonder if maybe you're taking on more than you can chew." Her eyes lingered on his package and he smiled "I know that you can handle yourself in that regard, but seeing me in my true form might be a little bit more than you can take. If for any reason you want to put the brakes on this, I will back off and you will never hear from me again. This is a promise that I will keep, so be aware that if I feel that you are scared or terrified for your life, I will take that as my cue to excise myself from the situation. I don't want to, but I think it would be in your best interest that I do, but that is of course if you can't handle the truth."

"Josh, this has been a bit of a shock to my system, but I guess we can only take one day at a time. The next full moon is in two days and that should be more than enough to tell me if I can handle this or not."

CHAPTER 8

"Sal, it's only about 3 hours until the full Moon and I can still go down to the basement and chain myself to the wall. Believe me, I don't want to do that and the wolf will become very agitated and want to take it out on the person that was responsible for putting them there in the first place. If you allow me to run free, I promise that I will never harm you, but I need the freedom to move and hunt like I normally do on any full moon. Feeling the wind in my fur and my eyes adjusting to the dark and the prey that is waiting out there for me is the only way that I know of giving myself freely to the beast within.

They had been together for the last couple of days and she couldn't even say anything to Anne, except to say that she was happy and that they were in the process of making a life together. Anne, being a good friend had decided to give Sal her blessing, but told her in no uncertain terms that if he hurt her in any way that she would castrate him with a pair of garden shears.

"Josh, I don't want to imprison you and to do that will only make you feel animosity towards me. Those chains would bind you, but your mind would still be fully alert and you would know that I was the one that was forcing you to do this." They were both dressed in casual sleepwear, with her wearing one of his shirts and smelling his scent. He was wearing a white pair of pants that was tied in the middle. There was no denying that they had this chemistry that made it almost impossible for them to go to sleep without screwing like never before. "You look so handsome and I'm very curious to see you change."

"I would rather that you didn't and that you remember me as I am now. When I change, I would rather do that in private and then come to you at the end of the night to find your comforting arms waiting for me." He was anxious, moving back and forth on both feet, fully aware that she was staring at him the entire time. If he really wanted to trust her, then she would have to see him in his natural form, but it was the initial change that he had found could be the most daunting to someone that didn't see it before.

He could count on his hands how many times that somebody had seen him change and each time was like they were out of their mind in terror. It was something that they could never unsee and would probably follow them around for the rest of their lives.

"Josh, if we're going to do this, I need to see you in your natural form." She saw that he was having none of it and it didn't matter how many times she professed her love, he just couldn't bring himself to inflict that kind of emotional damage to her psyche.

Josh felt trapped in his own skin and he could feel the prickling along his flesh, indicating to him that the change was imminent. "I have to leave." He went out the door and into the woods before she could do anything, as the first peek of the moon began to show itself through the medley of leaves in the distance.

She heard the unmistakable howling of a wolf in the distance and listened intently to hear her beloved raise his voice. She knew that it was him and then she saw a shadow looming and then a black mane of fur moving so quick that it was almost like a blink of an eye.

Taking a candle from the kitchen, she brought it back to the windowsill and lit it, essentially letting him know that she would be waiting for him. The wolf was now on the hunt and she was left feeling like she was being left out on a part of him. She would eventually have to tell him how she was feeling and what she had come up with as a solution to the problem at hand.

"My love and my everything, you have to know that I feel a certain piece of you is missing and I don't think I can do this without all of you being here." She went back upstairs, padding her feet on the wood, then clicking off the light as she made her way down to the bedroom. The window was open and she can hear howling, but it was further away than it was before.

Falling asleep, Sal awoke to make sure that the candle was not going to burn down the house, going down the stairs and looking out the window to see that same shadow from before was now lurking along the property. The wolf suddenly came into sight and they were now staring at each other.

She left him there, going back upstairs and crawling under the covers, not quite believing what she had just seen with her own eyes. It wasn't like he didn't warn her, but seeing it up close and personal like that was a little different. The reality of her relationship with him had now hit her like a ton of bricks, although she still was willing to fight for her man.

It was only a few minutes later when she suddenly felt like there was a presence in the room and she looked over at the clock to see that it was 530 in the AM. She glanced back to come face to face with the wolf and its angry looking teeth and eyes looking at her. She thought for sure that he was going to eat her or rip her part, but then his tongue extended and licked her face in this loving and nurturing manner.

Sal wasn't quite ready to see him change back, so she turned her back on him and made sure that she wasn't able to witness it.

Falling asleep, she awoke in the morning to see that the sun was now brightly shining and that it was well beyond 9:00 AM. It was only lucky that she had the day off and Josh hadn't really told her anything about his work or what he did for a living. From what she could get from their conversations, she thought for a moment that he was some kind of Real estate mogul and that he had talked about several properties that he owned. What she did know was that he was immensely wealthy and that over the years he had accumulated quite the fortune playing the market.

This left him with too much money to spend and very little time to spend it. He had already professed that he would like to take her away to some tropical island for a month-long vacation and she was seriously considering the possibilities of taking a sabbatical from her job as a kindergarten teacher. She couldn't put her finger on it, but there was something that Josh wasn't telling her. It wasn't so much that she knew it from what he was saying, but more from what he wasn't saying.

Every time that she had brought up anything to do with his childhood, he would shut down like it was a sore spot and she had respected his right to privacy. That part of him was closed down and she felt like she had to open him up and reveal that wound for what it was. Anything to do with his family was off limits and he would get this faraway look and soon he would be leaving the house on one of his long walks to clear his head.

Sal had a pretty good notion that Josh had already changed back to human form, but she just couldn't take the risk of seeing him as the wolf or something in between. She closed her eyes and listened to the heartbeat beside her, as if his heart was an extension of her own soul trying to reach out to touch her in a very subtle but meaningful way.

"No...you can't do this...STOP...she did nothing and it's me you want. NOOOOOO." She heard him scream this ear piercing decibel level that made her cringe under the bed sheets and what she wanted to desperately do was to turn and comfort him in her arms. She felt like such a coward for letting him go through that kind of turmoil without her by his side and feeling the strength of her arms as they encompassed his entire body. "I will go...but know that one day I will be back to exact my revenge on all of you. What you have done here has sealed your fate and there'll be no hiding from what I have in mind. You should've just killed me when you had the chance and you will regret that for the rest of your lives."

Sal heard his declaration of war, a battle that was out there waiting in the wings, but had no idea why this was to be. What had these people done to him that had made him so angry that he was so willing to risk being killed? Who was the woman that he had spoken about in his sleep and where was she now? Was he in love with her and was that relationship the reason why he was so closed off emotionally?" These were all questions that he was making her ask, but afraid to voice in his presence.

She lay there and waited, not moving and not wanting to disturb him from his deep slumber that he was in. He had already told her that after a hunt on a full moon that he would be too exhausted to move for hours and that he would probably sleep until well into the afternoon. That didn't surprise her, considering that he had been out all night and doing what wolves did. There was no telling what kind of trouble he had witnessed or come across in his travels and she thought that he would have so many stories to tell that there would be no limit. Unfortunately, he wasn't used to telling those stories and she saw it in his eyes that he wasn't willing to mention the things that he had done in the past.

They had talked several times and each time she would feel like he was pulling away, even though his arms were around her the entire time. There was no telling what secrets lay within his mind and what demons were waiting to raise their ugly head in the middle of the night in his sleep. The reason for his nightmares was because he couldn't bring himself to let her in long enough to get them off of his chest and she was going to have to do something to rectify that situation once and for all.

That man was now part of her life and whether she liked it or not, it entailed everything about him, including his past, present and future. That was something that they were both going to have to understand and Josh was going to have to make some confessions in order to rid himself of the guilt that he was feeling every single day.

"Josh, I don't know if you can hear me, but I want you to know that I am here and I am not going anywhere. You might not like it, but I am going to press you for more details about your past and I am going to do everything in my power to get you through this. You might hate me, but I think that it's best for you in the long run to get this out into the open." She lay there unable to sleep, waiting until the exact moment that she thought that it was safe to get up and go downstairs to get breakfast.

There was a knocking on the door downstairs and she couldn't even think about who it could be.

CHAPTER 9

Sal made her way down the stairs, while still looking up at the bedroom door where lies the man of her dreams. It didn't matter to her that he was something different than human and that once a month he would change to an animal. What he didn't know was that she was excited by that beastly part of himself, but she thought that it was wrong of her to feel that way.

"I'm coming...I'm coming...keep your shirt on." Flinging open the door, she came face to face with her best friend Anne. She was holding a bottle of wine in one hand and a can of tomato juice in the other. This had always been their ritual and Anne would come over and have Mimosa's and a late brunch when she had the day off.

"What fun is keeping your shirt on and I see that you have been a busy little beaver. His car is out in the driveway and he has been here for at least a few days already. It must be serious for you to shack up with him like this and I guess I can't blame you. He is one tasty looking dish, but I hope you are being careful and taking precautions. I'm not talking about sexually and I'm talking about how he broke your heart into a million pieces the last time he came around. Be sure that he is not going to do that again and if you don't mind I would like to have a chat with him before I leave here." Sal knew her tone and she was about to cut a switch off of Josh and make him realize that she would be standing in the way if he ever tried to hurt her.

"He was working all night and he's sleeping, but if he's awake by the time you leave, I don't see any reason why you can't have a conversation with him. Just go easy on him, because he has had a hard time of it as of late and I don't want to make anything more difficult." Anne saw that her friend was happy and she had no desire to rain on her parade, unless of course she saw that he was treating her badly. "He works nights one time a month and last night was that time of the month. I doubt that he'll be up until at least this afternoon."

"That's fine and I have all the time in the world and besides we still haven't begun drinking yet. Once I get a few into you, then I will grill you even more about his intentions." Sal knew that she was going to have to be careful with getting too inebriated, because she tends to talk a lot when she has a few.

"I think that I'm just going to stick with one drink for today, because I'm not feeling so well and I think it's better to feed a cold. Come to the kitchen and I will make us a couple of omelets from leftovers in the fridge." Anne followed her friend, watching for any sign that anything was amiss, but seeing nothing as of yet.

Sal was cooking and taking a sip of wine every so often, while Anne was still watching her from the table. "I thought that I smelled something delicious and thought that I would come down and help you. Whoa...sorry...I had no idea that we had company." They were both looking at him, but it wasn't because he was interrupting their girl time. He was buck naked, striding into the kitchen like he owned the place and wasn't ashamed of his body.

It didn't even occur to him that he was making them uncomfortable and Anne was taking everything in stride and enjoying the view. Her gaze followed to the object of her desire and she saw that he was sporting quite the package. Even soft, it was more than a match for some of the men that she had been with herself. "Josh, put something on before Anne has a heart attack."

"I have no problem with the way that he is dressed or not dressed as the case may be. If he has no problem putting it on display, then who am I to stop his free expression. Josh, why don't you sit down, because we need to talk before this goes any further. I need to know what your intentions are and please don't insult my intelligence by saying that you are in love with my best friend. If that's true, then why did you leave? It took a lot for her to just get dressed in the morning, but she never stopped thinking about you."

Josh stood up, went to the stove and wrapped his arms around the midsection of Sal "You've got nothing to worry about and my intentions are to make her as happy as she has made me. Just being around her has made me a better person and a better man. The man that she met last summer is dead and won't be returning. Sal has shown me that I can be happy and I am never happier than I am when I'm with her. I'm sure that you're going to say something about if I hurt her that you will hurt me and I wouldn't expect anything less." After they both said their peace, they sat and had a couple of drinks and shared a huge omelet that was meant for four people.

Josh tried to control himself, but he was famished from a long night of running and hunting. He took it back a notch, but he was still quite the feral animal. He did have the semblance of mind to use utensils, as he usually ate with his hands and didn't mind getting his hands dirty. The wolf and him were now one in the same and the worst traits of each of them had come out during the transformation to the wolf and then the transformation back to human.

"I still have my misgivings about this relationship, but as long as you keep her happy and glowing like she is right now, then I don't think we're going to have a problem with each other. I think that you are some kind of nudist and you didn't want to subject my friend to that kind of lifestyle. It appears that she has no problem and I certainly don't." she was licking her lips, but she knew that he was off limits. It wasn't even like he was her type, but that didn't stop her from ogling the merchandise. "I think that I should go and I've taken up more than enough of your time as it is." She motioned with her head for her best friend to follow her to the front door and then she hugged her.

"What's this for?"

"I just want to tell you that I was proud of you and giving him a second chance couldn't have been easy. I'll see you back at work Monday morning and I hope that you enjoy your weekend. I know that we promised each other that we would go for a hike tomorrow afternoon, but I will understand if you call and cancel." Sal couldn't have asked for a better friend and they parted ways and now Sal had a question to ask Josh.

Going back into the kitchen, she heard slurping sounds and saw that he was licking his plate clean. "Bad boy." She couldn't help herself and he had left himself wide open for that kind of retort.

"Oh, because I am some kind of dog, you think that you can treat me like that and get away with it." The chair moved, scratching against the wood, as he reached out like some kind of monster and chased her around the living room. "I'm going to get you." He lunged and found himself on top of her on the couch. They looked at each other and then they raced up the stairs giggling and going into the bedroom.

It was in the middle of the day and the sun was shining through the curtains with the sound of traffic in the distance. They frantically stripped each other and then went into the bathroom and turned on the shower. "I don't think I will ever get enough of you, Sal. I hope that I didn't put your friend out and I'm usually very comfortable around strangers. I guess it's the wolf inside and I didn't have this kind of confidence in the past. You would have never found me walking around my living room naked, but now it feels like second nature. You should try it sometime and it's very liberating without having all those clothes choking you to death.

They climbed under the hot spray and the water pelted against the wall, as they tenderly kissed with Sal still having that question lingering in her thoughts. "I have something that I want to ask you, Josh." He lifted her easily into his arms, her legs wrapped around his waist and his prominent member touching her sex.

"I think that any questions can wait until later." She wasn't about to say no, not when they were so close to boiling over with passion for each other. "I just can't think straight when you're around and sometimes I forget that I'm different. Then something happens that makes me see who I am and you would think that I had regrets. At first, I was terrified, but now that I have lived with it for so many years, I feel at one with the wolf and myself." Josh felt like he was at home in her arms and then as he thrusted into her womanhood, he knew that he could never be apart from her ever again. He had no idea how they were going to make it work, but the feel of her lips surrounding his shaft was more than enough to convince him that there had to be a way.

"Oh god...Josh...yes...that's it...take me." Sal found that she was losing all of her inhibitions, as the window was wide open and any of her neighbors could easily hear her cries of joy. That didn't even enter into the equation, because she couldn't care less what anybody thought and was quite taken by the fact that Josh had come back after all of this time. "Wow...oh my...CUMMMMMING." Throwing her head back, she felt immensely satisfied, but yet he had not joined her in his own expulsion.

Her body was begging for it, slipping up and down on him and grabbing at his manhood as it moved in and out of her at a rapid pace.

She was spent, a rag doll and he had to hold her up, while at the same time taking a couple of steps forward, so that she was pressed up against the tiled wall. He had his hands underneath the inside of her thighs, and his thumbs were rubbing her clit, as his arms were taken the brunt of her weight. It had no bearing on anything and the strength of the wolf inside him was more than enough to hold her steady. She felt powerless and yet ready for anything that he wanted to do to her.

"Sal, this is the kind of stamina that you will have to get used to and I never allow myself any kind of pleasure, until the person that I am with is fully satiated." Sal couldn't speak and was having her first multiple climax, something that she had always dreamed about but had never seen come to fruition. "The way that you're doing that is driving me crazy. I don't know if I told you, but I haven't been with a woman in some time. I always feel that I am less than honest and there came a time that I just couldn't do it anymore. Instead, I kept to myself and I suppose I was just waiting for the right one to come along."

"I can't...even...ahhh...ahhhh...speak." Sal, had her arms wrapped around his neck limply, but she still could feel the prominent bulge conquering between her legs.

"You're the best thing that has ever happened to me and I never want you to feel that I've neglected you or taken you for grant....AHHHHHHHHHH." gritting his teeth, he felt that imminent explosion and then it shot out of him like a volcanic burst. His climaxes were always legendary and he had to thank the wolf for enhancing his experience by a hundredfold. Not only had the wolf given him the stamina to keep on going when most men were exhausted, but it had also given him an oversensitive and intensified orgasm. It was like electrified wires were touching his skin and he wondered how he ever did without the wolf in his life all this time. "I love you, Sal and I would never ever hurt you."

CHAPTER 10

Sal wanted more than anything to see him change, but it took four months of them being together before she could gather the courage to put herself through that. The full moon had already risen and Josh had already left on one of his monthly excursions into the woods.

Staying awake, she watched TV and then read a trashy novel, making sure that she was not asleep when he arrived back home.

Falling asleep, she awoke; as the weight of the bed shifted and she turned to see the wolf licking his lips and then extending its tongue to lick her face and neck. It excited her to no end to feel this close to him in this form and then his eyes began to change, becoming dilated and then she saw the man behind the wolf.

If she had any doubts, she would turn away, but she didn't. In fact, she was quite enamored by the way that his fur suddenly began to pull back into his skin and then seeing his face contort into a mask of what could only be extreme pain and agony. He should've been screaming, but she instinctively knew that he was putting up a front on her behalf. His face came into focus and then his naked body was right there for her to see it up close and personal. Running her hands down over his sinewy flesh, she traced each individual muscle, coming to rest on the one muscle that she was most interested in.

Without a second thought, she straddled his lap and lined up his ramrod stiffness with her sex. Forcing it beyond the barrier of her moist center, she endeavored to take him all the way in before he could open his eyes and realize what she was doing. "No...I'm too tired for this, Sal." She wasn't listening and was now putting her hands on his chest and rising and falling with his cock coming out until just the head was inside her.

"Josh...Oh god, Josh. I've been meaning to ask you something and I think that I would like to be like you." She was riding him and watching his facial expression and hoping that he had been having the same thoughts. "I know that this is a big decision and it's not one that I take lightly by any means. I just feel excluded from a part of your life that is very much a part of you and I want to know you and the wolf inside. The only way to do that is for me to walk in your shoes and become a true couple with the same affliction and maybe have your children." She was in no hurry, driving down and then back up so slowly that it was almost excruciating for both of them.

"Sal, I really think that you've been getting caught up in the hype and you really don't know what you're asking. This life isn't easy and I wouldn't wish it on my worst enemy. How can I possibly do that to the woman that I love, when I know deep down inside that you will regret it and most likely hate me. That is not a risk that I am willing to take and I don't want to hear anymore...ahhh...ahhh...about it." He was exhausted, but that didn't stop him from putting his foot down when it came to changing another human being into the thing that he was.

He had strong feelings about this matter and it had been a contingent with some of his own kind over the years. He believed that a human being should have the right to choose, but some of his pack believed that the only way to keep the species alive was to recruit by force others into the fold. Josh felt like such a hypocrite for how he was thinking and he had built his life around the fact that he gave people the choice before he changed them. To him, it was a curse, but there were those that had changed that found the world that he lived in fascinating. It was those diehards that he sought out, because they would go into this with their eyes wide open.

He was asleep before she finished, but that didn't stop her from continuing her exploration of his flesh, until she felt the rising of his balls and then the flow of hot cum that made her smile on the outside as well as the inside. She had broached the topic, but he was in no condition to say much of anything, so she was going to have to bring it up again and as many times as was necessary to make him change his mind.

In the morning, she goes about her daily routine until he suddenly pokes his head into the kitchen for a cup of coffee. "I don't know what got into you last night, Sal, but you can't be doing that after I've just returned. I think the after glow of what I go through after the full moon is a little taxing on my body and you jumping me like that didn't help anything. I don't even know if I felt any of it, only that I awoke with your scent on my body. I know that you were just caught up in the moment and that you really don't want to be like me."

Sal couldn't allow this to pass, not when she was this close to getting what she wanted "Josh, I was very serious about my request and for you to take it lightly like that was a bit of a slap in the face. I've accepted everything about you and you have to accept the fact that I want to be like you and to live in your world. We both know that it's the only way to keep us from losing interest in each other and this way I would never be scared of you again. I think that is a small price to pay for continued happiness and the way that you shut me down was hurtful." She was standing her ground, once again wearing one of his shirts, as she just couldn't be without him for too long.

"I can't believe that after everything that you've seen that you would want to be like this. It means giving up your life, never living the same way again and always waiting for that full moon to rise during the month. Just tell me that you are joking and we can get past this, because I have no intention of inflicting this kind of hell on somebody that I love."

"Josh, you're being selfish and the sooner you realize that I want to be a part of your life in every way possible, the better off you'll be. It's not like I haven't given this some thought and believe me I haven't thought of anything else from the moment that you sprung this on me six months ago. We have been doing this dance and I have been hesitant to tell you my feelings, but no more. If you can't give me what I want, I will try to find it some other way and we both know that I am pigheaded and will never give up. Wouldn't it be better if it came from you and that way we could be together in human form and in wolf form? You can't tell me that you haven't thought of it before and I am giving you myself freely." She saw that he was shaking his head, slapping his own face and then looking at her like he couldn't believe that these words were coming out of her mouth.

"Sal, you're asking me to do something that I have strong feelings against and if we went through with this, there would be no going back. It's not like you can change back and before you do something that you regret, I want you to give it another couple of days. By then, I hope that you will see just what kind of mistake this can be. If not, I will reluctantly give in, but I will do it under protest. I still don't think this is a life for anybody and if I had my choice, I would rather be human than a wolf one time a month."

"I don't think you mean that and I've seen the way you light up when you become the wolf. It's like you are free for the first time and I want that same feeling for myself. No longer will I be shackled to the urban lifestyle, when nature calls to me. I've never been camping or out in the wilderness in my life, but I've always been fascinated by the sounds of wildlife. It's not just that and I told you before that I feel that there's something missing between us. I know what it is and you know what it is, but it's up to you to realize that this is the solution that works best for both of us."

Sal was pleading her case, opening herself up to ridicule and his unyielding attitude on the subject.

"Sal, I've lived this life for too many years as it is and I would give it all up in a second."

"I don't believe you, because if you could go back in time, would you really want to ruin this relationship by making sure that it didn't happen. The only way that we can be sure of is that we were meant to find each other. You could have easily bumped into somebody else last summer, but you bumped into me. The odds on that happening are astronomical, so you have to believe that somebody played a hand in putting us together."

"This entire thing is giving me a headache and you're going to have to give me some time to think about this, Sal." The full moon was near and they really only had 24 hours before he would change once again. This time Sal wanted to be a part of it and she could almost feel her inner wolf trying to break free of the prison of her own making. "Let's stop talking about this, Sal."

Josh was well aware about her feelings and he would be lying if he didn't say that he was curious about what it would be like to be with somebody of his own kind. He had tried that one other time, but it was a colossal error in judgment. He thought just because they were the same that they would be able to get along, but they were feral beings and were fighting more than they were making love. It was the reason why he had to leave the pack, because he felt betrayed by the wolf. After they had changed, the wolf inside him had killed the other one and he had awoken with blood on his hands and this guilt hanging over him like a Damocles sword.

CHAPTER 11

Josh changed that night, but this time he felt different like there was a piece of him missing. He couldn't put his finger on just what it was, and then he returned from the hunt to find that Sal wasn't there.

At first he thought that she had left him and his heart dropped when he saw the note lying on the pillow of their bed. With shaky hands, he reached for it, but turned away like it was on fire or something.

"Get a grip...you're a wolf...not a chicken." He was encouraging himself, not quite ready for the break up that was coming towards him like an oncoming semi-trailer. Finally, he braced himself, grabbed the letter before he could lose his nerve and stood there and read every single word twice.

It said "Josh, I've got some thinking to do and you really hurt me. I'll be back and I just need some time to think things through. This is hard on both of us and I know I should have just stayed and hashed this out. Please, forgive me, but know that I don't give up that easily. We're far from finished with this and I still have a lot to say and you're going to listen to me. Even if I have to hog tie you to the bed, you will hear what I have to say. Don't go to sleep, I'm just having a couple of drinks with Anne and then I'll be home." Josh couldn't believe what he was reading and it wasn't a break up letter. It was more of an ultimatum and he had never had anybody talk to him like that.

At first he wanted to leave, but his legs wouldn't work, like they knew that he would be making the worst decision of his life. He tried to go for the door several times, but still he couldn't do it. The worst that would happen is that he would listen to her rant and then reject it. Two could play this game, although he really didn't want to fight with her.

His anger and worry abated and he started to look at this from her point of view. It was his curse, but he did share it with her and now they were in this together for better or worse. In all respects they were in a committed relationship and when things got rocky he almost bailed.

The door opened about an hour later and Sal came in drenched from a downpour that just happened. Not even thinking about it, Josh raced to get her a towel and something hot to drink. He found her waiting at the bottom of the stairs and wrapped her up in the towel.

Guiding her to the kitchen, she sat down and watched Josh struggle to find the tea and it almost made her burst out laughing. He had no idea where anything was, but he was giving it his best shot. "You really don't have to do that, Josh."

"I know I don't have to, but I want to. Besides if it wasn't for me, you wouldn't have been out in that in the first place. I feel bad, so let me do something to make this right." He continued until he had the tea ready, stirring in the honey and then placing it on the table. "If you don't like it, know that it was my first time and I'll try to do better next time."

"So, there is going to be a next time and does that mean you've reconsidered?" She was half expecting him to blow up again, but instead, he sat quietly deep in contemplation.

"Okay, I'll do it, but you have to know that I don't know if this is right. I have to cut you and then myself. Then I have to place my wound against yours and that's about all there is to it." He sliced her hand with his own fingernail and then did the same to himself. The blood pooled together, as he pressed his against hers. "Initially this will be painful, but I know that you can handle anything."

"I'll be fine, Josh, and as long...as long...oh my...that was unexpected...AHHHHH." She heard somebody screaming and realized that it was coming out of her.

"Sal, hold on and I'm right here with you all the way. That feeling is your blood being changed and you just have to ride it out." She was gritting her teeth and she couldn't think of anything more painful. She hadn't gone through childbirth, but this had to be right up there. "You're doing great and you won't have to worry about the change until the next full moon.

"I....don't know if I can do this." Sal was gripping his arm, when her fangs emerged and her fingernails dug in to his hand. They retracted quickly and it was an odd sensation to say the least. "It feels like I'm being ripped apart...ahhhhh...from the inside out." All Josh could do was hold her and let the metamorphosis take place. It was over in an hour and then she slept for almost two days straight.

They talked about what happened and over the next 25 days, Josh prepared her for the change. He knew that nobody could really be ready, but having knowledge was better than going into it blind.

The moon was full and they stood naked together, as Sal felt her body change and her skin turned to fur. Her face morphed and she watched Josh do the same thing, until they were both down on their hind quarters.

Josh looked at Sal and they began to run into the forest, showing a little baby bump and the revelation that they were with child. They were going to be a family and they couldn't be happier.

Unfortunately, they weren't alone and found themselves being watched by a man with a scruffy beard and wearing hunter's clothes. He smiled and then picked up his cell phone. "I found him and you won't believe what he's been up to."

NEVER FORGOTTEN

Chapter 12

Sal for her part was having a wonderful time, frolicking in the woods and running around with her new paramour by her side. There was nothing that she liked more than feeling the wind in her hair or fur as the case may be, but feeling that growing life inside her was becoming a love that she didn't even know existed.

That first night, they hunted together and she found the taste of animal blood in her mouth so intoxicating that she became a feral beast in her own right. Tearing into the flesh and letting it nourish her body and the body of the baby inside of her was a bit of a shock. She didn't know that this was what he did, but she should've realized that running into the forest was not just for freedom alone.

They had looked at each other from time to time and it was in their mannerisms that they realized that they could talk without speaking words. All they had to do was nod their head or send a signal and both of them would know instinctively what the other was thinking. They were connected with his blood running through her veins and Josh felt a little bit guilty for letting her convince him to change her, but the die had already been cast. There was no going back and seeing that she was carrying his child, he really didn't want to.

At the end of the night, they returned home and crawled into the bed together, this time as wolves and then changing back to human form and looking at each other naked and vulnerable for the first time. "I hope you know that I still have my reservations about this, but I am just too damn exhausted to get into an argument over it." He felt like somebody had run him over with a truck. There was no denying that this transformation was taxing on both of their bodies and he was worried that something would happen to the baby.

He needn't have worried; because Sal was doing everything she could to protect the little one, even going so far as to avoid too much strenuous activity. As a wolf, she could let herself go, but with this new life, she had to be aware that anything that she did affected the fetus. "I don't think I gave you a choice and basically I gave you an ultimatum and you chose wisely. Believe me, I've given this a lot of thought and even after the change, I would say that my decision was the right one. After all, there was no way that we could be a true family without living in each other's world. That was the thing that was missing from this relationship and now that piece of the puzzle has been put into place." Josh still wasn't sure and Sal was the only one that he had turned in quite some time.

There were two others, but they were distant memories at best. One was a female, not a lover but someone that had gotten in between a deadly fight between him and another wolf. Instead of letting her die, he felt that he had to do something for her and gave her the healing abilities of his blood to make herself whole again. He had been keeping an eye on her from afar for some time, but she eventually disappeared altogether and he was left with a very sinking feeling that he had done her wrong. It might've been more kind to let her die in her own way and he believed that his sin was not hers to carry.

As for the other one, he really didn't wanna think of him, as they never saw eye to eye from the very beginning. The man was desperate; clinging to a hope that something was out there that could save him from a fate worse than death. He was dying of a disease and it was a slow process, something even the doctors couldn't understand.

It wasn't until this man came to his doorstep one day that he found himself faced with a question of conscience. That was 10 years after the woman and that particular mistake was now just a dull ache in his stomach. He tried to tell him and that he shouldn't do this, unless of course he had all the facts before trying such a thing.

""Josh...earth to Josh." He came out of his memory, looking at his bride to be and the ring that was affixed to her finger. She was showing puzzlement and then he noticed that he had gotten lost in his own thoughts. "I know that you carry a lot with you, but I'm now a part of this and I'm here if you want to talk." Sal could see that something was bothering him, something from a long distant memory that had come creeping back into the forefront. "This is no longer a one way street and we now live as one." The Josh that she knew last summer was nothing like this man and in that time he had hidden all those things that haunted him.

"It's nothing to worry about and I was just thinking about something that I did that maybe I shouldn't have. I'm not talking about you, although I still think that it was wrong for me to change you like that. I should've giving you more research, allowed you to become fully aware of what you were getting yourself into. It was your passion about doing this that made it impossible to say no." Josh could feel her naked body against him and touched her skin to feel this electricity that was forming like an invisible barrier around them.

He had never felt anything like this before, but he had heard rumors of such a thing amongst his own kind. It was said that a human woman would be the perfect host to their kind, because it would allow the baby to enjoy both sides of the same coin. It would be a child of wolves and humans alike. There had never been anything of the sort, at least as far as he could remember. It could've been that there were others like him that had gotten caught up with a human female before realizing that their heart was stolen from the moment that they laid eyes on them.

"I know you say that, but there's something in your eyes that tells me differently. I won't pry, but just know that I would never divulge anything that you say to me. Anne still doesn't know about my transformation and I don't think it would be right for her to know this part of us. I will tell her about the upcoming child and nuptials, but in the end I think that she needs to believe that we are just a normal couple. That could change down the road, but I really don't see any circumstances that would make me want to reveal this to my best friend."

"Sal, I won't tell you what to do; only that humans have a hard time dealing with things that they don't understand. My kind has been hunted in the past and there are factions of Frankenstein type doctors that want to examine us up close and personal on their slides. That was a long time ago, but I'm sure that there are still those that are out there that still want to find out what makes us tick." He wasn't telling her something, a secret that went beyond just the fact that he was a werewolf. There were things about him that he couldn't tell her, unless of course he wanted to risk losing her altogether.

"That's terrible and I don't see why people are so shortsighted. I guess I was a little bit taken back and the moment that you changed in front of me was life altering. I thought that I was dreaming and that I was just trying to make something up to explain why you had left so long ago. Last summer you captured my heart and I now see that I have done the same thing to you. This night has been magical, but there were times that I thought there we were being watched." She wasn't sure she should voice her concern, but maybe this was what being a werewolf was all about. It was possible that she was just feeding off of her own adrenaline and it could've been due to the new and wonderful acute senses that came with being a wolf.

"You know, I was going to say the same thing, but I thought that I was just paranoid. Now that you've said something, I am beginning to think that we should be more careful. It could've been a hiker or somebody with a digital camera. In this day of technology, we have to be more aware of our surroundings, because anybody at any time could come upon us and videotape us. Even cell phones are now capable of shooting video and I would say that being a wolf is more dangerous than it has ever been before."

No longer could they run freely, without first taking in their surroundings and making sure that nothing was going to see them. This was going to take a conscious effort on both of their parts, but as long as they were together, there was nothing that could shake their resolve.

"I guess you're right, Josh. Now that we are having this baby, we can't take chances like that anymore. If we were to be captured on video, there would be no telling what would happen to us and the child. Like you said, we as humans are not exactly comfortable with things that we don't understand and we tend to lash out." Sal had seen her fair share of movies and those that were considered different were outsiders at best. How was she going to raise a child normally, when during the full moon he changes into something that would be considered a monster to others? Now she was rethinking her decision, but once again there was no going back.

"This is going to be difficult, but it could be a whole lot worse. We could be changing every night, instead of just once a month during the full moon. One day isn't going to kill us, but it does mean that we will have to be vigilant from now on."

"Josh, like you said, we are in this together and as a family we will deal with this together. In the meantime, I think that we should get some rest, as we have a big day of checking out caterers and finding me a wedding dress. I really don't want anybody to know that I am pregnant, and I don't think it's going to be easy to hide. This kid is growing by leaps and bounds and if I didn't know any better, I would say that I was at least three months into the pregnancy."

"Yeah, well that is how these things go and his supernatural abilities are allowing him to form quicker than the normal child. I will say that once he is born that you will have a healthy baby boy and for the most part he will grow up like everybody else. The only time that his development is heightened is in the womb. Outside in the real world, his metabolism will slow down and he will only begin to feel that he is different at his 10th birthday. Then again, I've never heard of a human female giving birth to one of us, so this could be all conjecture on my part."

They curled around each other, naked and warm, but still smelling of sweat and pine needles from the forest. His hand swept across her chest and grazed her nipples, just enough to awaken those sexual senses that had been aroused during play time outside. They didn't try to have sex that night, because they just didn't have the energy in them to jump each other's bones.

When they fell asleep, the man that was holding the binoculars outside put them away and climbed behind his black wrangler jeep. He was wearing camouflage clothing, easily hiding and always one step ahead of the wolves. His crooked smile showed that he was up to no good and the way that he licked his lips, almost made him look like he was some sort of hunter after its prey.

CHAPTER 13

“I don’t care and I won’t be bothered by such nonsense. Be gone and never darken my doorstep again or face my wrath.” A man wearing a robe and a long white beard is being administered by a couple of doctors that are not exactly finding their new patient cooperative. “Stop touching me and get your needles away from my arm, or I swear that I will rip off your head and drink your blood.” They were taken aback by his proclamation, but they knew that he was not of right mind and didn’t really mean what he was saying.

“Lucas, you have to take your medicine and we have to take blood work in order to find out what is happening to you. It’s not normal to have all of your organs shutting down for no good reason. We’re trying to make a protocol that is going to help you, but you insist on fighting us every step of the way.” He received the back of Lucas’ hand against his face. It made him stumble back and he touched his cheek to feel the wetness of the blood that was now taking shape.

“This is none of your business and I don’t see how you got past the guard. My son will have to answer for this and you better be out of my sight by the time that I turn around from the window or else.” His tattered old brown robe billowed around his naked form, as it was not closed and he wasn’t at all ashamed of his frail body.

Instead of getting into another fight, the two doctors that were present decided to make a discreet exit. They did have a little bit of blood work, but that was from when he was sleeping. It was going to have to do, because right now this man wasn’t going to let them get anywhere near them without some kind of recompense.

“Father, you really should try to get along with the doctors, because they are only trying to help.” The man that was watching the wolves was now stalking his father, who was standing at the windows looking at nothing. His gaze was almost trancelike and he had his hands behind his back like he was some kind of dictator to be feared. "This is for your own good, but I do have some news on that other matter that we discussed." Even this didn't wake him from his fugue state, but the next words were enough to summon enough control for him to break loose of the prison of his own making. "I found him."

Lucas turned abruptly; grabbing Reginald by the throat and looking at him from all angles before letting him go. Coughing, Reginald looked at his father, but still saw that there was no real semblance of him in there anymore. He was losing the battle for not only his sanity, but for the ravages of this disease that was taking him one piece at a time. It had been a long and arduous process, but eventually his death was inevitable.

"I don't like when you joke like that and we both know that he has been hidden for over 25 years. He was the one that did this to me and had he finished the job, we might not be in this boat. I've had so many people looking for him and yet you come to me out of the blue and tell me that you've found him. Tell me, son, when others failed, why is it that you succeed? You're not exactly the most capable person and sometimes I regret having you. You don't have the killer instinct that is needed to get the job done, but now you stand here defiantly and tell me that you've found him. Why should I believe anything you say, especially when you bring these doctors around to make me feel like a pincushion?"

"I know that we have a strained relationship and I won't take it personally that you just told me that I was a mistake." Reginald was tempted to just keep all of this to himself, because after all, his father would be dead soon and the empire that he would leave behind would be his to rule. Business was not his forte, but he did well with hunting and fishing, something that his father had never taught him and he had only learned because of his uncle.

"Stop beating around the bush, kid and tell me what you've found. Let me decide if it's worth you barging in like this and interrupting my solitude. The only enjoyment I get any more is staring out at the window at the water below. The lapping of the waves keeps me calm. Don't think for one second that I don't know that you want to inherit all of this. Since you are my only son, I have no choice but to hand over the reins to you when the time comes. Before that happens, I want my revenge and the only way I'm going to get it is if I can find Josh."

"Josh has been hiding in plain sight this entire time and we had no idea. I've been following news clippings of wolf sightings and each time that something unusual happens like an animal being torn apart, I put a pin in it and then do my own reconnaissance. Last night, I came across him and he was no longer hiding in the woods, but was actually keeping house with a woman. Not only that, but she has a bun in the oven. I don't think I have to tell you what this means, because your salvation could be at hand."

The old man picked up a glass and threw it at his head, barely missing it by a couple of inches as it sailed past and crashed into the fireplace. "Josh isn't stupid enough to get involved with a woman and he has always said that he wanted to keep this part of his life to himself. Those times that he came close to finding love, he would walk away before it became anything more than just a small spark between them. If you are telling me the truth, then he has gone against his word and his moral code. Then again, I really don't care what he does and I only want to see him groveling at my feet for his life." The old man couldn't believe his good fortune, as he really thought that he was going to die before he got his hands around Josh's throat.

"If you want, I will get him and bring him back here, but that is up to you to decide. I know that this has been weighing heavily on your mind and on your body and you might want to do with this on your own. I would say that you were in no shape to exact this vengeance, but I now see a sliver of light in your eyes that wasn't there before."

"Reginald, you might just be a good son after all, but I do believe that this is my fight. That's not to say that I don't want back up, because he will undoubtedly fight me tooth and nail. He thought that he had given me a gift, but it has only been the bane of my existence from the time that I received it. I think he was too young at the time and he really didn't know what he was doing. That is the reason why that I feel this way and the full moon last night was excruciating. I won't bore you with the details, but changing from wolf to human every hour on the hour is not my idea of a good time."

Lucas went to the patio doors and threw them open with such haste and determination that the glass shattered upon contact with the outside furniture. He stepped over the broken pieces, not even caring that the shards were digging into his skin, until he was leaning over the railing with his fist in the air in triumph. "I'm coming for you and you better have your affairs in order and believe me I haven't forgotten about your little bitch and bastard. You'll watch as they die first, as I take everything from you and make your life the living hell that mine has been for the past 25 years."

Reginald was touching his beard and heard everything that his father was saying, but he knew that his father had no idea that he was even in the room anymore. He was talking to himself and for no good purpose than to utter a threat to somebody that had long been considered dead and buried. He had only recently found out that his death was faked and digging up his grave three months ago, he came to the revelation that Josh was not 6 feet under.

He had come to his father with this new information, only to be chastised, until finally he showed him the proof.

Once he saw the proof with his own eyes, Lucas couldn't deny that the man that had put him into this condition was still out there somewhere. He couldn't allow that man to live, not with what he had done to him. If anything, he deserved the same fate, but he would contend himself with ending his life with his own bare hands. If it was the last thing he ever did in this life, he would kill everything that he held dear and then turn his wrath on the man himself.

Reginald didn't like how his father treated him, but he did have this desire to help the old man find some closure. His tirades were getting a little tiresome and there were times that he wanted to smother him with a pillow. He even stood over his bed with the pillow in hand, wondering what it would be like to hear him gasp his last breath and smiling the entire time.

When his father told him when he was old enough that there were such things as werewolves, he began to research heavily on the topic. He found werewolves to be fascinating and he had even captured a couple to do a more in depth examination of their physiology. His father had no idea that he was a werewolf fanatic, nor did he have any idea that he had medical skills. From the time that he was 10 years old, Reginald began to see that his father was deteriorating and knew from his long winded stories that it had something to do with a man named Josh.

He had no ill will towards Josh and he probably did him a favor by making his father a shell of his former self. There were times that he thought that he was going to beat him to death when he was a child, but now that he was feeble and weak, he couldn't even lift his own hand. He could intimidate with words and manipulation, but the real threat of any immediate harm was gone.

This man was not the same as the man that had used him as a punching bag, but in that same regard, he had become the man that he was today because of it. He didn't back down from any fight, no matter how big the opponent and there were times that he had learned to fight dirty. "You seek out your revenge, father and then maybe you can finally rest in peace. I know that you've been holding on this long because of this insane idea that you could kill the man responsible, so I made it my life's mission to find him for you."

He saw his father standing at the railing and he had to look away because the robe was not exactly keeping things hidden. This was a sight of him that he didn't need or want to see and if he could he would've scratched out his own eyes to prevent it from happening now. There was something about him that was different and ever since that he had told him that he had found Josh, there was a new light in his eyes. Something dark had taken a hold of him a long time ago, but now his life had new meaning.

As he watched him, he began to think that maybe it wasn't such a good idea to find Josh, because there was no telling what he was going to do once he laid eyes on him. His strength had waned considerably over the years, so doing this himself wasn't going to be easy. That didn't mean that was going to stop him, because Reginald had learned a long time ago that once his father had something in his head, there was virtually nothing that anybody could do to stop him.

CHAPTER 14

Just watching her sleep was nirvana and now he understood some of those old country songs they had been playing on the radio. His heart was now hers and even though he didn't like staying in one place for too long, he had found something that was worth the risk. It was a risk, because what he had done in the past shouldn't involve her. Unfortunately, she was now a part of his life and whether he liked it or not, she was going to hang on for the long-term.

This woman had been in his thoughts for too many months to count and every day he would think of her and her smiling face. To be lying here with her and her as a newly formed werewolf was a little bit more than he could wrap his mind around. After all, he hadn't intended to come back here and destroy her life or do anything that would cause or harm.

Sal wasn't one to back down and it became quite obvious to him that life without her wouldn't be living at all. It didn't matter that she wanted to be a part of this life, because he could never say no to any of her requests. He still didn't like the idea of her being this way, but now that she had taken on the transformation and the baby was well on its way to being developed, he could see that she was quite rubinesque. Not that that bothered him at all, because he liked her anyway that he could get her and besides there was more of her to love.

"I know that you're watching me and I find it very sexy that you would want to watch me sleep, but also a little unnerving." Sal had been awake for a few minutes, but she hadn't ventured to open her eyes yet, only knowing that she was being watched this entire time. He was leaning upon his elbow, staring at her and smiling and that in itself had made her feel wanted and loved like never before. "This baby has certainly put the pounds on me, but if I don't say so myself, I think I look pretty damn good. All it did was make my breasts even bigger and give me that full figured look. I really didn't think that I was going to like it, but I have to say that I enjoy the new curves. It's not that hard to tell that you like the way I look, but I know that you're not that type of guy."

He was moving his hands up and down her soft belly, feeling the kid kick for the first time and almost jumping out of his skin when he realized that there was really a living person inside her. Moving to put his ear against her stomach, he felt the kid kick again and this time with a little bit more force and determination between bursts of energy. They had slept for 12 hours, not moving or doing anything at all, but now they were awake and ready to fulfill their duties as parents.

"If you're asking if I am some kind of chubby chaser...the answer is no. I do admire a woman that doesn't mind putting it all out there for everybody to see and I kind of find it sexy that you have those qualities yourself. There's nothing that you could do that would make me love you any less. From the day we met, I knew that we were going to find a way back to each other, but I had no idea when that would be. It's just that I couldn't control my need to see you and I guess I'm at fault for bringing this to you."

Sal could feel that he was regretful of his decision, so she had to do something to tell him in no uncertain terms that it wasn't all his doing. It wasn't like he had a choice and she made it quite clear that if she didn't become a part of the werewolf lifestyle that he would find her leaving him in the middle of the night. "This has always been a two way street and it wasn't like I was giving you any other option. If you hadn't done it, I would've found somebody that would, no matter how long it took and then I would've come back to you. It's just lucky that you didn't make me resort to those measures, because I really didn't want anybody to turn me but you."

"Sal, there's no way that you could've done this without me, because there's no way that you could've found anybody. You wouldn't have the sixth sense to seek them out and if they found out that you were looking for them, they might do something more extreme than just turn you. They could have killed you, so I guess I am happy that you convinced me to do it for you. Now that we are a family, I do believe that we have a few errands to run and you have to meet Anne in the next 20 minutes. While you're gone, I'm going try and put the baby's room together. It shouldn't be all that hard, but I just hope that I don't run into complications. I hate to see words like put this in slot A and I would rather do it with my own bare hands than go by any kind of directions."

"Typical man, when things don't go your way, you decide to go it yourself. They've been too many instances in time that a woman has said 'are we lost' and gotten the reply 'no, we should be there any time. It's not that we're lost; it's just that we don't know where we are. I would rather you wait for me, because I have a knack for putting things together. A few of my friends have kids and I was quite instrumental in putting together cribs and other assorted furniture. I have quite a reputation for doing it and every time that somebody is about to have a child, they would always call me and get me to put the furniture together before their husbands could wreck it. I guess I just have a keen eye for detail and I instinctively know where each piece goes without looking at the directions. It's all about shapes and geometric formations and I can see it in my mind's eye as clear as ever."

Sal never knew where she got this particular talent, because her parents were not exceptional in building things. It had to be a gene that was passed down from another part of the family and she knew that there were many in her family that had this creative genius running through their veins.

"Sal, you don't give me enough credit and I think that I can handle it on my own. I'm going to have to get used to doing these things, because he will have to have a bicycle put together when he gets older and I would like to think that I am the man of the family. It wouldn't make me look very good if you were doing everything that I should be doing, so for this I'm going to have to put my foot down." Josh was looking at her and hoping that he would convince her to leave this to him, only to see that she was crossing her arms in defiance, most likely not very happy with given an ultimatum.

It was one thing for her to give one, but it was entirely different matter altogether when it came to him doing the same thing. Men were notorious for trying to get their way, always trying to assert their authority and always finding that the woman was more than a match for them. “Tell you what I’m going to do and this is all that I’m going to hear on the subject. I'll let you try to get things ready and you have until I am finished with talking to Anne about my wedding dress to get things done. If it’s not done by then, I will have to take over the project myself and I don’t want to hear anything more about it after that.” She was very opinionated and didn’t mind showing that she was a strong willed woman.

“That will be more than enough time to get things together. I’ll show you that I am worthy of being your husband and father to our child. In fact, I intend to take on some of the duties of diapering and I don’t want you to think that you’re going to have to do this alone. I’m not your typical man and I don’t shirk away from my fatherly duties. It doesn’t matter to me that I will be up all hours in the night, because I’m a bit of a night owl. I suppose we both are now and you’re going to have to get used to the fact that you might be waking up at 3:00 AM and not be able to go back to sleep. That’s the wolf inside you and even though she won’t come out until the full moon, doesn’t mean that the wolf doesn’t control a little bit of what you do.”

He knew that he should’ve told her all of this before they had decided together to do this. Going into this blind was never a good idea and sometimes things go wrong. His mind conjured up the images of a young man that had come to him in a moment of great need. He wasn’t even fully a werewolf, only being bitten a couple of months before that, but his humanity was still intact and he wanted to help this man.

“I never said that you weren’t man enough, I just said that you were stubborn like most men. You would never ask for help, but if you are not finished, you’re going to get it whether you like it or not.” She was already on the floor, lifting her weary bones onto her feet and then going over to her closet to look at clothing that couldn’t possibly fit her anymore. She was going to have to find a whole new wardrobe, but for the time being she did have this outfit that was left over from a party back in 2003.

When she put it on, she felt him reaching around behind her to snap the buttons into place. It was essentially a very loose fitting yellow and white dress. The only reason why she had it was because the party in question was themed cross dressing and a lot of men had come dressed as their favorite character. Whoever had been wearing this was quite the big boy, but for some reason he had left it behind during the night.

Sal really didn't think that she would have an occasion to wear it, but for some reason she decided to keep it nonetheless. It was in the closet all this time and just gathering dust, but now she was wearing it with pride and holding her child with both hands and leaning back on the shoulder of Josh to hear his heart beating in his chest.

"You look absolutely delicious and if we had the time, I would crawl underneath there and give you something to think about." As it was, she was feeling his hands touching her breasts, which was unencumbered with a bra. The way that he was touching her made her feel like she would swoon into his arms and fall headlong back into bed. She let out this involuntary sigh and closed her eyes to the pleasures that he was inflicting on her.

Josh couldn't help himself, because there was just too much of her not to want to touch, not to mention the huge presence that had only been there a few days at best. At least, the dress in question hid the fact that she was pregnant, but how long they could keep up that ruse was anybody's guess. "You're just saying that because you have to."

He turned her abruptly and made her face him "I would never say anything that I didn't believe and just wait until you walk down the street and feel all those eyes behind you. Each man will want to be with you and you exude this open sexuality that none of them will be able to deny. It's a byproduct of the pregnancy and your hormones are now raging out of control. That means that your pheromone levels are off the charts and right now you have the ability to sleep with any man that you want. It doesn't matter that they find you attractive or not, because your natural scent will draw them to you like a moth to a flame."

"You have nothing to worry about and I have only eyes for you. It does make me feel good that they will see me as a desirable creature and not a fat woman." They hugged and he followed her downstairs wearing just his boxer shorts, which of course wasn't keeping anything under wraps. Even as they open the door, a female was jogging by and had to stop for a moment and tie her shoe under the pretense of looking at the large object that was now trying to make its way down the left side of his boxers.

They were kissing and had no idea that they had an audience and his excitement became more prevalent until the head of his cock was the poking free from the leg band. She couldn't help but stare, but at least she was wearing mirrored sunglasses to hide the fact that she was looking at Josh like he was some kind of prime steak.

When Sal walked by her, she noticed that the woman's nipples were poking obscenely through her shirt and she had to smile knowing that Josh had this effect on every woman. Then again, she was beginning to see that his assessment of her condition was right on the mark. Every man that was about to get in their car to go to work was now stopping everything that they were doing and watching her. She made a point to smile at them, wave to them innocently and then bounced up and down for their amusement.

CHAPTER 15

"My god...what the hell have you been eating these last few days. When you told me that you had a big surprise, I had no idea that you meant that you were trying a new look." Even in the coffee shop, Sal was aware that the men were trying to be nonchalant, but their gaze was on her the entire time that she was sitting there. Some of them were doing a better job of hiding it than others and those that weren't were getting a swift kick under the table from their respective companion. "I know that you've been seeing Josh, but I thought with all the sex that you were having that you would be more svelte."

"What can I tell you...I eat when I'm happy and Josh likes me just the way I am." She raised her hand and wiggled her finger, showing off the engagement ring that he had given her in the middle of the night. The ring was a family heirloom that was passed down from generation to generation and she felt a bit of pride for wearing it on their behalf. "This is what I wanted to tell you and I was hoping that you could help me find a wedding dress in the next three weeks. We don't want to wait and we've been alone and apart for way too long as it is. When you know it's right, you know it's right and we both know that we found our soul mate."

"You really don't waste any time and of course I would be happy to help you find a wedding dress. I hope that you would consider me for your maid of honor, but then again who else would you ask. We've been friends for way too long for you not to give me that responsibility and you know that I would never do anything to ruin your big day." Inside, she was a bit jealous of her friend's happiness, but that wasn't going to stop her from supporting her and giving her a shoulder to lean on. "There's a beautiful spot down the street from here and we can walk and talk at the same time. I personally know the owner and she will give me a discount on everything in the place. If we can't find something that will complement your figure, then we aren't doing it right. Don't worry about anything, because the owner is a good friend and she has a keen eye for detail. That's the reason why she got into the business and she has this need to make people happy all the time. It was a little annoying growing up, but her choice of profession really does suit her to a T." The green eyed monster was there, but she couldn't tell Sal how much this was hurting her inside.

There was no significant other in her life and she had nothing that was serious or looked like it was going to turn into something more.

"I know that this is asking a lot, but there's nobody that I would want by my side during this time. You have been with me through all of my milestones, including my graduation and even getting my job as a kindergarten teacher. It has been one hell of a ride and I guess it was inevitable for one of us to get married. I'm just kind of sad that we won't be walking down the aisle together. I know you say that you're happy with your life, but can you honestly tell me that you don't want something like this for yourself."

"I would be lying if I didn't say that I was a bit jealous, but I'm just happy that you found the one that you were meant to be with." The fact that she had gained 30 pounds in the past few days was a little of a concern, but she was glowing so much that it was almost like a neon sign was over her head saying that she was pregnant. If she had to make her guess, Anne would have to say that her friend was trying to keep the pregnancy quiet. That way they could get married with respect and not have a shotgun wedding that made it look like they had to get married instead of wanted to. Why she just couldn't be honest was making her a little miffed, but she could certainly allow her the right to privacy.

They finished having their coffee and then began their short walk down the sidewalk. They weren't alone and there was a man smoking a cigarette across the street in a nearby black Corsica. Every so often, he would raise a long lens camera and take pictures of both women. He was given an assignment and he wasn't going to risk having the wrath of the old man come down on top of his neck. Lucas had become increasingly difficult to live with as of late, but Karl was just happy that he was in his employ. He couldn't make this kind of money anyplace else and even his unpredictable mean streak wasn't enough to make him run the other way.

They just entered a nearby bridal boutique and he had gotten a close-up shot of her displaying the ring for her friend. There was no way that he was going to be able to go in there without being seen, so he was going to have to stay out here and wait patiently for them to come back out. Lucas wanted everything documented, photographed for later use and didn't care about the cost. This was the type of employer that he had always dreamed about and even this small job was going to bring thousands of dollars into his bank account. He looked into the mirror and saw that his bald reflection was quite alarming and losing his hair in a matter of months was a little bit more than most men could take. The nice thing was that he could pull it off, but even so, he had been going to the gym as of late and putting in a work out that would make most men fall unconscious at the end of the day.

He had seen many celebrities with this same affliction and could see that they had put on the muscle in order to feel at ease in their own skin. Reginald was the old man's son and Karl always thought that he was a bit of a mama's boy, but he had seen with his own eyes that his dislike for his father was quite evident in the way that he looked at him. It wouldn't surprise him at all that the old man would die one day at his hands and that the son would take his rightful place at the head of the table. Karl had always been a big believer in keeping his friends and enemies closer, so he had done everything he could to make Reginald see him as a sort of lieutenant.

His phone began to go off in his ear, as he was wearing a blue tooth system that allowed him to go hands free. It helped with his job and it didn't hurt that it was fashionably stylish as well. "I have her under surveillance and I've been following her ever since that she left her house. I left my partner to stay at the house out of sight and she is posing as a jogger and should be able to keep that cover for at least a couple of hours. Don't worry about a thing and by the time I get back, you'll have a better understanding about this relationship and the man himself." Karl didn't really have a partner, but he did use the services of Nicole from time to time. The girl was a bit of a chameleon and could become practically anybody that she wanted.

He had met her at one of his jobs and apparently they were working the same case from opposite ends. They become fast friends and had even finished the job so that both parties were paid quite nicely. It wasn't sexual and they never crossed that line, but that didn't mean that he didn't think of her in that way. Actually, she had been feeding some of his fantasies as of late and he couldn't get to sleep without taking matters into his own hands with images of her bouncing around in his head. It was the perfect relationship and it was all about monetary gain and nothing else.

He had seen Nicole become anything from a nun, postal worker or even a teacher to get into places that were relatively secure. Sometimes he thought that she was carrying him, as he was older than her at 45 in contrast to her relatively young age of 23. Why she got into this kind of work was a mystery and he tried to pry it out of her, only to be shut down almost immediately.

Inside the boutique, Sal is trying on wedding dresses, making sure that Anne doesn't see her hidden secret. The only person that knew was the boutique owner, who had come in to help with a fitting and smiled and gave her a nod of congratulations for her condition. "I know that you are friends with Anne, but I would hope that you would respect my privacy and keep this little bit of information to yourself. I would think that discretion is a part of your duties as the owner of this place and I'm sure that this isn't the first time that you've seen a woman getting married that was pregnant. To put your mind at ease, I will tell you that it has nothing to do with why we're getting married, only that it makes it all that much better."

"I'm just here to help you with the fitting and nothing more. Why you're getting married is none of my concern and I respect that you know what you're doing. I think that Anne would understand and to not tell her anything is doing her a disservice. I've known her for some time and she is the least judgmental person that I have ever met in my life. She has always been kind and supportive and would give you the shirt off of her back if you asked her to."

Just standing there with this dress on, she felt like a princess and then she remembered that her prince was a werewolf like herself. Ever since that they had gotten pregnant, she was thinking about the child and what kind of life they could possibly give him. It had become quite the worry for her, even though she was keeping it to herself, when she probably should've been telling Josh how she was feeling. It was possible that he could've been feeling the same thing, but the only way to know was to voice her concerns and let the chips fall where they may.

"Anne, what do you think of this one?" Sal stepped out of the dressing room, preparing to model this latest creation, but instead of seeing her friend, she was accosted by an elderly man that was barely able to hold himself up with a cane.

"Anne stepped out to get a cup of coffee for the both of you. I hope that I didn't startle you and in your condition you shouldn't be doing anything that would harm the child." Before she could stop him, he was already touching her belly and looking up at her with a look that she just couldn't distinguish. "I thought that we should meet and discuss our mutual friend in private. Josh and you are going to be very happy together as a family and I imagine that soon you'll be hearing the pitter patter of little werewolf paws on the floor of your house." He actually said the address, making her cringe and begin to think that this man didn't exactly like Josh all that much.

"I don't know what your problem is with Josh, but this is neither the time nor the place to say anything against him. There is nothing that you could say that would make me want to leave him, so coming in here and trying to intimidate me is never going to work. You've wasted your time and I will marry him and have his child." He grabbed her by the wrist and for an old man he had surprising strength.

"I don't like the way you're talking to me little girl and I would hold your tongue if you knew what was best for you and this child. I've been nothing but civil, but believe me that can change very quickly. Don't make me do something that we both will regret and all I want to do is talk to you about Josh. This attitude of yours is making me mad and believe me you don't want to see me when I get mad. There are things about your soon to be husband that you need to know about, but then again I don't think he's going to be alive long enough for you to go down the aisle. He has a lot to answer for and you just tell him that Lucas wanted to give him his blessing. He'll know what that means and I imagine that you'll see his whole demeanor change when you mention my name."

"Is there something that I can do for you?" The clerk was little surprised to see the old man grabbing onto her client, but instead of shying away from adversity, she decided to step into the middle of things. "I think that you should leave before I call the police." What she received was a glaring expression that made her blood run cold.

"I'm leaving, but believe me this is not the last time that you'll see me. Josh and I were meant to have this final confrontation and this pregnancy doesn't change a thing." He wanted to send a message to his good friend, so he punched Sal in the stomach and watched as she doubled over in pain. "I could've done a whole lot worse than that, but I have something special for Josh and his soon to be family." Lucas wanted to kill her, but doing it without Josh as an audience was never going to give him the satisfaction that he was looking for.

He turned and abruptly left the boutique, knocking over displays of dresses and slamming the door behind them with the bell ringing incessantly over the door. Sal was breathless and said "I think something is wrong with the baby."

CHAPTER 16

Sal was in terrible pain and she looked at the clerk to see that she was in some kind of shock. It appeared that she was not going to be any use to her, but then she snapped out of it long enough to go to the telephone and call for 911. It was then that Anne came back with a coffee and dropped them summarily at the threshold to the store.

"What the hell happened?" She rushed over to her friend, very concerned and holding her hand as she lay back onto a chair that was nearby. "I just left for a few minutes to get some tea for you and coffee for myself. I come back here and find you like this and I have to wonder what brought this on in the first place." Anne could see that her best friend was in trouble and she wanted to do something to alleviate her pain. To that end, she found a cushion and put it against her back, as she had heard from her sister that this would help the baby to adjust.

Yvonne the clerk didn't know what to do, so she stood around and went towards the door to make sure that the ambulance would know where to go. This was the only thing that she could think about, because she didn't want to even entertain the idea that Sal would lose the baby in her store. That kind of publicity could ruin somebody and she didn't want to be selfish, but this was her livelihood. "I called for the ambulance a few minutes ago and it should be here momentarily. I think the only the thing we can do is try to make her as comfortable as possible and hope that this isn't very serious. That man had no right to do that to her and I should've gotten a license plate, but I was too stunned by his behavior."

"Yvonne, who is this man that you're talking about, because when I left here the only people inside the store were you and Sal? I need to know everything and I don't want you to leave anything out regardless if you feel that it is unimportant or not." At the time, Sal could not speak, concentrating on the baby's well being and breathing slowly in order to keep herself calm. "If anybody did this to her, they will have to answer to me and my five friends." She was referring to her fist and she wasn't above punching a man in the face or going after his genital region. Sal was her family and even though they didn't share a bloodline, didn't mean that they didn't have a connection that went beyond any other kind of friendship.

"It was an old man with a cane and I didn't hear exactly what he said to her, but then he grabbed her by the wrist. That was when I intervened and he gave me a look that could've killed, before saying that he was going to leave and then he punched her in the stomach. I think I heard him say something about tell Josh that Lucas said hello or something like that. I would say that the father of this child has some explaining to do, but for the time being I think that we should concentrate our efforts on keeping your friend from worrying. It's been my experience over the years that mothers tend to worry incessantly about their child in the womb and it's that very worry that could be the cause of the stress their body is under."

"Yvonne...after we get her to the hospital, I want you to show me the camera footage of this man. I know the police are going to want to get a statement from you and I want to see this camera footage before they get their hands on it." She was already envisioning her own type of revenge, a baseball bat in one hand and a bag of rolled up pennies in the other. She could already see the look of surprise on the old man's face when he felt those pennies slam into the side of his face and then the baseball bat take out both of his knees.

"That might be tricky, because the camera in the store is a dummy and is only used to prevent robberies from happening. It's basically a deterrent and nothing more, because I really couldn't afford anything else. It does look real enough and that has been a great help in making criminals aware that this place is under surveillance. I'm sorry that I can't do much more, but I could give you a very detailed description of him. In fact, I've been known to sketch from time to time and I think that I can get a pretty good likeness."

Sal could only listen to what they had to say, unable to interject her own thoughts because she was having trouble breathing. She was desperately worried about this child and she would never forgive herself if something happened to it because of something that she did. Even if this had something to do with Josh, didn't mean that she shouldn't be able to take care of herself. She was strong willed and didn't bow down to anybody and for that man to get the upper hand on her made her angrier than anything.

"I'll get you something to draw on and I think that I remember that you keep a notepad behind the counter." Anne began to rummage through everything in back, coming up with a pad that was already showing the outline of the morning outside these windows. "I'll have to take a look at your portfolio, because I have a few connections that might be able to get you a show. In the meantime, sit here and sketch the man's face, because the police and the ambulance will be here very soon. I hear the sirens in the distance and if they don't get caught in traffic, they should be arriving anytime."

Yvonne felt so stupid for not doing anything, standing there like a deer that was caught in the headlights, unable to move or call for help. Eventually, she came out of her stupor, but it was too little too late as far as she was concerned. If Sal lost the baby, she knew that she would feel the guilt deep down into her very soul for the rest of her life. There'd be nothing that she could do to take away the pain of that loss to Sal. She would never be able to look her in the eye again the most likely would get lost at the bottom of a bottle.

"I think that is the least that I can do under the circumstances and I should have a rough drawing of his face before the police get here to take my statement." She picked up a pencil and began to make the outline of the man's face, remembering that it was long and oval and he seemed to have a cleft in the middle of his chin. From there, it was all about the eyes, the nose, the mouth and how his hair looked.

She was usually about sketching scenery, but that didn't mean that she couldn't sketch people. There were some of her friends that had specifically asked her if they could get her to make a portrait, but nothing had panned out. Each time that she came close to doing one, something would happen to take the opportunity away. It didn't matter if it was a death in the family, an accident or something along the lines of a vacation, it was always something.

Anne knelt down beside her friend, comforting her and soothing her with her hand on the back of hers. "I know that you're scared, but there's no reason to be. Just believe that everything is going to be OK and I'm right here with you the entire time. Just look at me and we will get through this. I know you didn't want to tell me about the baby, but I already knew. It wasn't hard to guess and I've had a few girlfriends and even family members that have shown signs of pregnancy." Sal really didn't care if her friend knew, because she was just happy that she was there with her through this ordeal.

"I'm almost finished, but it's not like I'm Rembrandt and I would say that this is a rough draft at best. It will give you a basic idea of what he looks like and I think that is all that you'll need to track him down. I'm sure that the police will be able to use this same drawing and I'm going to go to the bathroom and photocopy it, so that they have one copy and you have the other." Yvonne felt so stupid, but at least she was able to do something that would hopefully find the person responsible for doing this.

"I just find it remarkable that you would have that kind of talent, because without it, I would be basically blind. It would mean that I would have to contend with what the police found and they wouldn't take it as seriously or personally as I would. I doubt that they would give it the priority that it needs and it would probably fall on the shoulders of somebody that was green instead of a veteran on the force. I have some friends that might be able to expedite this matter for Sal and I don't have any problem reaching out to them. I haven't talked to them in some time and they might feel a little taken back by my request, but they know that I can find every skeleton in their closet." Sal was listening and was seeing a side of her friend that she didn't know was possible. It was a vindictive and destructive streak that came from her fear of somebody coming after somebody she loved.

"Don't do anything...call Josh...please." Her words were whispered, because she didn't want to over exert herself.

"Oh, believe me, I am going to have a long talk with Josh about this and from what I've heard from Yvonne, it appears that he is the one that is responsible for bringing that old man into your life. Whatever happens to the baby falls on his shoulders, but I'm not going to get into that with you right now. It will only make things worse and I would rather keep your calm and breathing deeply." There was no time for I told you so, because the health of the baby was paramount.

"Not his fault."

"Sal, I'm not going to argue over this, because it's pointless and I really don't have the energy to make my point clear. Just to say that I don't trust that man and there's more to him than meets the eye. In fact, I think that there is a secret that the both of you have been carrying for way too long and maybe you have to let me in on it. After all, it appears that I might be able to be of some help, but I won't be able to do anything unless I know the entire story from beginning to end. Think of me as a psychiatrist or therapist and that whatever you say to me stays between us." She had this unique instinct for things and even last summer, she suspected that Josh was a little different than most men. Other men wouldn't be able to draw her into them like he was able to.

It wasn't even that he was trying, but he was doing it and she could feel it all the way through her body. It was like she had no control over her own faculties and there was a moment that she wanted to reach out and grab him in the not so subtle way. He wasn't even her type and she tended to gravitate towards those that were more muscular and had issues with their father or siblings. There was danger all around this man and if it was any indication of what happened to Sal, then he really did need to stay away from Sal and the baby. If she had anything to do with it, she would lower the boom on Josh and tell him in no uncertain terms that he had to disappear from her life forever.

She would promise to raise the child, but with him there it could only be more dangerous than if he were to vanish in the middle of the night like he did last summer. It would hurt Sal terribly that she had anything to do with it and she was going to have to keep this arrangement between the two of them to herself. Even if she had to dip into her own savings to bribe him to go away, she had no problem doing that for her friend.

The paramedics arrived and Anne took her copy of the sketch that Yvonne made and stuffed it into her purse before the police could be aware of what she was doing. The paramedics worked on her, taking blood pressure and doing all sorts of tests that would show what was happening to her.

"Excuse me for one moment, as I have a phone call to make to her fiancé. In all the commotion, I forgot that he needs to know about his baby and the condition of him or her. Let me give him a call and then I will be happy to answer all of your questions." She wasn't at all surprised to see that the officer in question was somebody that was young enough to be her son. This kid looked like he had just gotten out of the academy the other day, still wearing the starch uniform with his gun shiny and new strapped to his side. The one thing she did have to admit was that he was in great shape and she thought about seducing the young man into her bed.

"Don't be too long, because I know that it's best to get these things out in the open when they are still fresh in your mind." It was like he was talking from the manual, something that he was taught to say when he came across a witness. "Just keep in mind everything that was said and done and you have to try to envision it in your head. That way you won't forget anything and you can replay it like a movie over and over again in your head." He wasn't telling her anything that she didn't already know. This wasn't her first time being questioned by the authorities and she had a stalker back in the day that had gotten a little too close for comfort. Unfortunately, the stalker didn't realize the ball buster that he was following and soon found himself on the receiving end of a beating that lasted for at least 10 minutes.

Anne was a scrappy fighter and didn't mind fighting dirty and before long she was dragging this culprit into the police station on her own. She was chastised by the police for her vigilante justice, but their questioning of the suspect came on the heels of the beating. As it was, he was ready to talk and didn't want anything to do with Anne. Each time that he turned in her direction, she would glare at him and make him feel that he was nothing to her.

Sal was taken by ambulance and Anne made the call to Josh, only this time it was to the answering machine at the house. "Josh this is Anne...Sal is on her way to the hospital. Meet us there, because I have a lot of questions and you better have some answers." She finished her statement of fact, went over to the police officer and gave him a copy of the sketch. Along with that, she had arrived at the conclusion that she would have to give a statement as well and had already prepared it before he had arrived. Yvonne also had her statement prepared and all she had to do was sit down with the officer and go through it step by step.

"I think I have everything I need and I will be in touch if I have any more questions. I'm sorry for what happened to your friend, but this person will not get away with it." He was still green, always wanting justice and never fully realizing that sometimes justice was blind. This was his first case and his partner was outside sitting in the car watching everything go down. He was essentially grading him and watching for any errors. He didn't think that he was going to find any, because his brother was a police officer and his daddy and grandfather had served on the force as well.

It didn't matter to his partner, because he didn't believe in nepotism and wasn't about to give this kid any reason to make a mistake. His life was in his hands and he had to believe that this kid could back him up when the chips were down.

"If that's all, I would like to get to the hospital as soon as possible. Maybe you could use your siren to get us there quicker." It was now time for this young cadet to decide if he could bend the law. "Come on...think of it as a woman that is in labor and needs to get to the hospital in a hurry. She is sitting in the back of your car, breathing heavily and the head is crowning and you hear her screaming all the way there." She was painting him a vivid image, something that he could see without meaning to, until finally he nodded his head that he was willing to do that.

"My partner is going to have my head, but a promise is a promise. Follow us and I will get you to the hospital as fast as I can. If you want, you could come with us and that way we could cut down the traffic. Our sirens should be more than enough to push them aside." The young man was looking at this cougar, wondering if it would be appropriate if he had the balls to ask her out on a date. "After you are done, maybe we could have something to eat or go for coffee somewhere."

Anne enjoyed the fact that he was confident enough in his manhood that he was willing to ask her out. It may have not been the most appropriate time to do so, but it did show her that he liked her and that was more than enough to take him up on his offer. The proposition to have coffee or dinner with him was appealing and she actually thought about what it would be like to strip him naked and look at his naked body before doing anything with it. She was a visual creature, but she knew that most men were the same as she was, which basically gave her a leg up on the competition.

"I should slap you for that kind of comment, but you're cute and I don't mind saying that I wouldn't mind getting to know you better." She stepped up to him and pushed her breasts up against his chest, letting him feel the nipples poke into the fabric of his uniform. There was something about the uniform that was making her hot and she didn't realize that she had this kind of affliction until right this moment. "This is just a reminder of what is waiting for you when we finish this unfortunate business. I do hope that Sal's baby is fine, because if not, I would say that that would put a damper on any kind of date. Then again, if everything is fine, then a celebratory drink wouldn't be out of the question."

"That's the best news I've heard in a long time and I guess moving to this town wasn't such a bad idea after all. My family might not like it, but sometimes you have to do what you need to do for yourself. My father at least understood that being in the force meant that you had to take any position that was available. It was possible to get back to your own home town, but sometimes it took years and sometimes you never actually made it back. Now that I've met you, I can say that things are looking up."

His words were like soft velvet and Anne felt instantly attracted to this man. At first, she thought that he was naïve and too young for anything more than a spanking, but he had proven that he was more of a man when he had asked her out. They exchanged information and she found out that his name was Zachary. It would be interesting dating somebody that was younger than her, but this wasn't her first rodeo when it came to bagging a cub. It would be her first time trying a relationship with somebody like him, because most often than not, she would do unspeakable things to them and in the morning send them away with teeth marks in their ass.

"I'll give you a call either way, but even if we can't get together tonight, I don't see a reason why we can't get together in the near future. Let's not get ahead of ourselves, because we still don't know the condition of my best friend and until we do everything is in the air." She'd already followed him out to the car, climbed into the back seat and could hear rough mumbling coming from upfront. She couldn't hear what was being said, although the man that was his partner didn't seem at all pleased by him bringing her into the car.

CHAPTER 17

Sal arrived at the hospital and the nurses and doctors were so kind and before long they found out that the blow to the kid was not as significant as it was once thought. She was lying there on the gurney in the emergency room with an IV in her arm just to be on the safe side and a panel of tests that were being conducted to make sure that everything was perfectly fine with the baby.

"I don't want to hear it and only thing I want you to say is that you will leave her the hell alone and go back to where you came from. This is all your doing and you should be ashamed of yourself for putting your fiancé in that kind of danger. Don't even think for one second that you can backpedal with some kind of excuse, because I know for a fact that someone is looking for you and doesn't mind sending a very poignant message to get your attention." Behind the curtain, Sal could hear her friend taking a stitch off of Josh, but so far he hadn't been able to get a word in edgewise.

"I didn't..."

"Stop lying to me...you fucking coward. If you want to make amends, tell me who this Lucas person is, where I can find him and then let me do what needs to be done." Anne had already called for reinforcements and her Cousins were more than happy to lend a hand. They had taken the sketch that was given to them and was now sending it around to the pipeline in order to ferret out this man's location. It wouldn't be too long, except of course if he had come from out of town, and even then it was possible that one of her contacts at the Airport or even the local hotels would know something. "That woman loves you with all her heart and she has been pining for you ever since you left her the last time. Now that you're back, she doesn't want you to leave again, but I am not under that same impression."

"Okay, I will tell you that I'm not Lucas' favorite person. I did something that I regret, but instead of sticking around to find out how everything went, I left him to figure it out for himself." He felt so bad for what he had done that he sort of understood why Lucas was taking these measures. That didn't mean that he wasn't going to do something about it, because it was high time that the two of them came face to face after all of these years. He had only done what he thought was right at the time, but it had turned out to be a monumental mistake. He probably thought that he had abandoned him, but he had been searching for something to rectify the situation, only coming up empty handed. It was then that he decided to leave the situation; pretend that he had died and even staged a funeral in his name.

"That's not enough and you have some explaining to do." She was poking him in the chest with her finger, making him back down and move back a few steps. He could've easily detained her, knocked her out, but he just couldn't bring himself to do that to somebody that Sal called family. "She is fighting for your child and for you to stand here and do nothing makes me want to punch you. I'm not talking about some common slap from a woman, but instead a real punch that comes from bending my fingers and reeling back with everything I have."

"Look, I appreciate that you care for your friend, but she is my fiancée and maybe you should stay the hell out of it." He didn't want this constant backbiting and he was getting a little annoyed at Anne sticking her nose in his business. "You were the one that was with her and why didn't you do anything to protect her. I've heard some of the stories from Sal and it's not like you can't take care of yourself. Unless of course you weren't with her at the time, which means that you feel as the guilty as I do for not coming to her aid in time." Josh realized that he was playing dirty pool, because he had just turned everything around to make it look like it was Anne's fault.

"I will take some responsibility, but ultimately it comes down on your head, Josh. Do something about it, because if you don't, I will and believe you me he won't know what he is messing with. I didn't like seeing her doubled over like that and I had this red hot rage come over me, so much so that I had to take a couple of deep breaths. It's a good thing I did, because I wanted to do something and since I couldn't get my hands on the old man, I was going to turn my wrath on you instead."

"I need to see her and you standing here and preventing me from doing that is only going to cause more problems." She was standing her ground and Josh made one move and was now behind the curtain.

"Please...don't...fight She's my best friend and I would like...for the two of you to....get along." Sal thought that was wishful thinking, because Anne was very opinionated and would come out fighting if something bad happened to her family or friends. In this regard, Sal was considered both of those and there were times that Sal didn't know what she would do without her. "This is hard enough as it is without the two of you constantly fighting like a couple of children. If you can't get along, at least be civil long enough to get me through this and then you can go back to fighting like cats and dogs."

"I will try to make a truce with her, but I don't think that she is going to be very accepting. That woman is something else and it would be a damn shame that I would ever come toe to toe with her in a fight. I just see her as somebody that would fight without honor, especially when it came to protecting or defending the honor of you."

"I know the two of you are scared. Josh, but the doctors told me that the baby is perfectly fine. The punch apparently knocked him out temporarily, but it's nothing that a few hours of deep slumber inside my belly won't cure. They are doing some tests to make sure, but they're reasonably certain that I can leave here in an hour or so. It will be nice to get back home and take a hot shower and relax. I know this has something to do with your past and I'm afraid that I won't be able to rest until you at least tell me what the hell is going on. Believe me, I don't have any judgment and whatever you did back in the day is in the past and has nothing to do with you and me." Sal wasn't quite sure of that, but it was the only way that he was going to open up to her.

"Let's just get you out of the hospital first and then I'll be happy to answer any of your questions. Just remember, I am not the same guy that I was back then and the things I did might seem a bit extreme at first glance. I was always trying to do good, but there were times that my efforts were in vain. He kissed her, listening to her heartbeat slowing down to a manageable level and even the machines that were peeping incessantly began to subside. It was the calming influence of the wolf that was making the most difference and without it; the baby could've been in real jeopardy.

"No, you'll just stall again and I think it's about time that you put all the cards on the table. We can't go on like this and whatever this man thinks you did, it's about time that you step up and do something about it. Besides, I don't think he's going to go away and I think the only reason why he didn't kill me and the child was because he wanted to do it in front of you. It was in the way that he looked at me and in the way that he spoke of you that made me believe that revenge is a dish best served cold in his opinion. The doctors want me to rest for the next couple of days and that means I can't have somebody trying to kill me every 5 seconds."

Anne walked in and she was stopped by Josh's hand. "This has nothing to do with you and I would appreciate it that you let me talk to my fiancé in private.

"I think that anything that you have to say can be said in front of my friend. We've hidden the secret from her, when I knew in my heart that I should just be honest. It doesn't matter if she believes us, only that we get it out in the open where it can't do any more harm." Sal wasn't sure that Anne would be willing to listen to any of it, but this was no time to be squeamish.

"I just want to go on the record that I think this is a very bad idea, but if we're going to do it, I would rather do it some place more private than inside this hospital. For the time being, I will say that this man has a right to hold a grudge and the axe that he is carrying will be sharpened to an edge. It has been many years since we've seen each other and he blames me for his condition. I thought that I was helping, but I had only made things worse. I will say that it seemed to work at the beginning, but then things began to change and there was no going back. As a werewolf, I bit him, because he was dying of an incurable disease and this was the only way that he saw that would allow him to see the next day."

"A werewolf...are you kidding me with this. We ask you to be honest and you come up with this harebrained notion."

"Let him talk, Anne."

"You're not buying this...but you are...aren't you?" All Sal could do was level her gaze at her friend and let her know through the connection that they had together that he was telling the truth. "I can't believe this and what kind of brainwashing has he done on you? I would think that the both of you would know that something like that is not possible." Anne was trying to be the voice of reason, but they weren't having any of it. She looked at the both of them and they seemed to be communicating without saying a word. That was something that only she and Sal was able to do, but it seemed that Josh had that same connection... maybe even more so.

"Anne, Sal wanted to tell you, but I convinced her that I thought it was a bad idea."

"That's not entirely true; Josh and I thought it wasn't a good idea myself. I guess I got it in my head that us humans are a bit more skeptical and I had to see with my own eyes before I even contemplated such a thing. Now that I am one of them, I see things clearer than I've ever had before. Once we get home, we can show you, but there's no way that we can do that in here."

"I could show her enough to make her curious." With that, he looked at Anne, grabbed her by the shoulders and seared the yellow eyes into her brain.

Anne saw his eyes change color, but thought that it was the trick of the light that is until she looked more closely and saw the wolf trying to get to the surface. "It can't be...and you're both just fucking with me and I don't like it one bit."

"Anne, Josh left me last summer because he thought that I couldn't handle it, but now that we are a family, I have no intention of backing down from anybody. This wolf has claws and I and the baby have no problem using them to protect ourselves and those that we love. This might be hard for you to understand, but I would hope that you would keep an open mind. We have been through too much to let this tear us apart and besides I think that we could use your help. You've always been good at finding people and I've never asked you how you did it and I don't intend to ask you now. I would ask that you put out the feelers and try your best to get a location for this man. We need to have a discussion and it has to happen on our turf."

"I still don't believe any of this and I don't think anything that you say is going to change my mind. Even the trick with his eyes is not enough to convince me, and you're going to have to do a whole lot better than that. If this is true, then a full moon should be just what it would take to prove it and I believe that one is coming up in the next 15 days. If you really want to convince me, then I should be there when you make this miraculous transformation. If that happens, then I will have no choice but to believe you, but until that happens, I'm afraid that I will have to remain on the fence. I will however track down this old man and I don't care if he's a Mormon or a wolf, because nobody treats my friend like that and gets away with it. A man should never put their hand on a woman and for him to do that only makes him look like a coward in my eyes."

Josh had some kind of spell over her friend and she was going to do everything in her power to break it. If that meant that she was going to have to play along for the time being, then she had no problem dancing to their tune.

"I think it's time that you get me out of here and back home where I can be safe. Why don't you go to the nurses' station and get my release papers and I will make an effort to get dressed. Don't worry, I will be careful and take no unnecessary risks with my health or the health of my baby. This life is too important and even though I don't know what kind of mother I am going to be, I will lay down my life in order to keep it safe."

"I feel the same way and this kid is going to have so much love that it won't know what to do with it. It will even have a very gutsy and determined godmother, but that's if she's willing to take on that responsibility. I don't usually agree with you, but having her on our side is a good thing. She is fearless and will stand up to practically anything without being afraid or trying to run away. We couldn't have chosen anybody better to be his godmother."

"I was going to ask her, but I was going to wait for a little while. Now that the cat is out of the bag, I don't see any reason to wait any longer. Would you do us the honor of being his godmother and will you protect him and teach him everything that he needs to know that we haven't?"

"I still don't know a about this, but I could never say no to you, Sal." She didn't even address Josh, because right now he was persona non gratis. Until this matter was settled between him and the old man, she would not trust anything that came out of his mouth ever again. "I will do it and it would be my honor."

He left them alone, but only for enough time for him to go to the nurses' station and inquire about her release papers.

"While he's gone, blink once to tell me that you are being held against your will or blink two times if he has brainwashed you in some way. Does he belong to some sort of cult and is he their leader and does he promise to bring them to nirvana?"

"Anne, you're being silly...he's not keeping me against my will or brainwashing me. In fact, I think that this is the healthiest relationship that I've ever been in for a long time and I would hope that you would be happy for me. Regardless if you don't agree with what he's done, doesn't mean that you can't act normal when you are around me and him together. If you can't do it, then fake it, because I really don't care one way or the other. He's a good man and he will provide for me and the baby and give us a good life together. You would never be out of the picture and it doesn't matter that we don't see eye to eye on this."

CHAPTER 18

After leaving the hospital, Sal and Josh went back home, as Anne had some errands to run and left them with a promise to stop by in the early evening to discuss things.

Anne still couldn't wrap her mind around the fact that he was calling himself a werewolf and she was going to have to give them some harsh truths when she saw them next. If they thought for a second that she believed their story, then they were sadly mistaken. In fact, she was going to do some research and disprove their theory, unless of course they could change into these werewolves that they spoke of. She had no doubt that they had delusions and even though she saw his eyes change, she really did chalk it up to the fact that the light was hitting him in just the right way.

The errand that she had to run was research on Josh and she had a friend at a local newspaper that owed her a few favors. This might be exactly what she needed to uncover Josh's dirty little secret, because she was nothing if not persistent. She could stay cloistered in the bowels of the newspaper building for hours, looking over old clippings and trying to find any sign of Josh.

"You know that I'm going to get in trouble for this and you better make it worth my while."

"Andy, you know that this is a quid pro quo kind of relationship and right now you're the one that owes me the favor. How soon we forget about my spying on your ex in order to get ammunition for your divorce. I think those telling photographs that I took from a distance were more than enough to garner me a few brownie points." Anne could see that Andy wasn't bad looking, kind of young, but she was beginning to think that maybe going that route wasn't such a bad idea. She'd always fancied younger men, but mostly they had become a second thought after the act. There was this one man on the Internet that she was corresponding to, but so far it hadn't gotten further than a few sexual innuendos and some flirting.

"Don't remind me and that bitch almost took me for everything I had and then some. You were instrumental in giving me back my life and I suppose I can turn my back for a couple of hours while you go downstairs. I might even forget to lock up and leave the key on my desk by accident." She watched as he turned his back to her, giving her the opening that she needed to go downstairs and begin her research.

3 hours into searching, and she found nothing about Josh that went back more than 20 years. It was as if he didn't exist before that time, but everybody leaves some kind of environmental footprint in their wake and Josh couldn't be any different.

She heard what sounded like a squeak and then footsteps slapping against the concrete. "Andy, if you are trying to scare me, then you're going to have to do a whole lot better than that." There was no answer and she decided that it was just her imagination running over time. After all, these old basements make noises, what with the pipes being old and the building shifting with age.

Continuing with what she was doing, she finally found an obscure note about a young man that was supposedly bitten by a wolf. On further examination, she noticed something familiar about the man, but she just couldn't put her finger on what it was. She peered at it for a long time, looking for any clue that would lead her to believe that she knew the person.

A couple of hours more went by and yet the only clue that she could find was that picture of the young teenager. They said that it was a miraculous feat that he had survived, but then something else happened that gave the family hope for the future. Apparently, the kid was dying of some kind of incurable disease, yet after the bite and some antibiotics for infection, he suddenly bounced back to a normal teenager. Soon after that, he disappeared, not more than a couple of months after his recovery. She just couldn't get over the fact that this kid looked familiar and there was something about his eyes that gave her room for pause.

"Hmmm...I do believe that you've stuck your nose into something that you shouldn't have. I come down to places like this all the time and to see you here has only raised my curiosity. It also makes me wonder why you are looking at the same material that I have been looking at in various cities and newspapers for the past few years." Reginald, the dutiful son of Lucas had found many instances of wolf bites and that was the only reason why he had found Josh in the first place.

"You scared the hell out of me and now you have only raised more questions than answers. If you are looking into Josh as well, then you must have some kind of connection to the old man that accosted my friend this afternoon. I'm not one to judge, but if he ever lays a hand on her again, I will end him. In fact, if you come anywhere close to me, I'm going to make you regret it." Anne felt powerful and she knew that a man would be foolish to try to go against her. She was well proficient in Tai kwon do and was taking classes to master the art of self defense. Not only that, but she also carried a taser and pepper spray, just in case somebody tried to attack her on the sidewalk or going to her car.

Her safety conscience came from a friend that had died from a mugger that was looking for his next fix. That made her begin locking her door and looking over her shoulder to be aware of her environment at all times.

Reginald raised his hands n mock surrender "Relax little lady, I have no interest in getting into a fight over something that is none of my business. I only search out these answers for my father and yes he is the old man that probably came face to face with your friend, Sal. If I were you, I would stop digging, because once you go down that rabbit hole there is no coming back. Don't say I didn't warn you, because once you learn everything you need to know, there is no taking it back. I learned that the hard way and you can imagine my surprise when some of those Revelations came to light."

Anne noticed that this man was rugged and manly, a little rough around the edges, but nothing that she couldn't shave off. He had this sense about him, an awareness like she did and he was constantly moving his eyes from one corner of the room to the next. It was like it was second nature, something that was in bred in him and his psyche. It had to come from his upbringing and his father and she had to give some thought to if this man believed anything that went along the lines of a werewolf.

"Before you go, I need to know if you believe in werewolves." She saw him change demeanor and then he pointed at her before turning on his heels and leaving the same way he can. "Wait, you didn't answer my question." She pushed the chair away, hearing the squeak and moving towards the door, only to see that there was nothing there but the sound of the air conditioner.

Meeting Reginald was unexpected, but it did open up her eyes to something that she had been missing. Going back to the same article about the child named Jackson L; she suddenly realized that the L stood for Lucas. She knew that it was in the eyes, but the strange part was the date on the newspaper was a little weird. The old man that she had seen on the drawing couldn't be more than 65 years old, yet this article was in print back in 1900. If this was true, then the old man shouldn't have been born yet. Puzzles were usually Anne's pastime and putting this one together was something that she wasn't going to stop until she finished.

The altercation between her and Reginald had shaken her, but it wasn't anything that a nice shot of vodka from her hidden flask couldn't cure. The young kid in the photograph couldn't have been the same old man, because if he was, then her entire out look on the world was going to change drastically.

Taking the flask, a silver memento that was given to her by her grandfather; she touched the cold surface, turned the cap and then poured the liquid gold into her mouth. It danced on her palate, where she savored it, until finally it moved down her throat. She wasn't an alcoholic, but she did enjoy a couple of drinks before work and after. She gathered up everything that she could find, going over to the photocopy machine and making copies of everything. When she had this arsenal in her possession, she left the basement, went back upstairs and used the key to lock the door behind her. Come to think of it, it was already locked, so how did Reginald get down here.

It didn't matter, because she was going to use the key and then leave it in Andy's desk, so that he would find it in the morning. She would have to take him out to dinner sometime to thank him, even though this was a favor that he owed her. It didn't matter, because their friendship was built on doing things for each other, but also on the fact that he had been there from the moment that her mother was diagnosed. Not even Sal knew about her mother's condition, because she just didn't want to burden her best friend with her own personal problems.

She began walking down the hallway towards the exit, hearing the click and clack of her heels against the dark linoleum floors. Then she had the feeling that she was not alone and turned to face a fist that crashed into her face.

"I don't know what we're going to do about Anne and she's going to be here in the next 15 minutes to talk to us. We will have to have her over in order to prove to her that werewolves do exist." Sal didn't relish that date, but they had already paved the way with telling her that they were now werewolves." She felt his hot breath on the back of her neck and then felt him nibble on her ear. "Stop that...you're driving me crazy." She's really didn't want him to stop and secretly hoped that they had enough time to go upstairs and let nature take its course.

"I know you're worried, Sal, but the genie is out of the bottle and there's no putting it back in. We're just going to have to deal with this together, head to head and if she doesn't want anything to do with us after the change, then we're going to have to accept her decision. I know that's hard for you to grasp, because she has been your best friend for as long as you can remember." He loved her and the curves of her newly formed body was making him salivate at the chance to get her into bed again.

Their sex life was amazing and any time they got together it was an explosive combination of two bodies coming together. Now that they were both wolves, they could have sex as humans and as wolves. As humans, it was more tender and loving, but as wolves it was more feral and out of control. It was a nice contrast to mix up from time to time and that wild side was an aspect of sex and they could tap into as wolves. It had only been a little while since they had changed together for the first time, but it felt like it was forever.

“I am worried and I don’t want to lose my best friend over this. She has been with me through everything and even during my breakup with you, she was right there to pick up the pieces and help me move on. She knew that I could never get over you, but she did everything she could to keep my mind occupied on something else. If she wasn’t around, I’m not sure if I could’ve survived without her, which means we’re going to have to do everything we can to convince her to keep our secret and stay in our lives.” Sal knew that this was going to be hard on Anne, but if anybody had an open mind it would be her.

Wrapping his hands around her large belly, he knew that it was probably going to be a quick birth and most likely would take place on a full moon. A birth of a werewolf baby could only take place in werewolf form and he had already told her all of this and she had taken it with a grain of salt. He knew that she wasn’t happy about a wilderness birth, but she accepted the fact that this was how it had to be. If they could do the same thing for Anne, then he wouldn’t feel like he had destroyed the one relationship that had stood by her through thick and thin. That kind of guilt could destroy a person and he didn’t want that weighing heavily on his shoulders.

Her thoughts were interrupted by the ringing of the phone. It reminded her of how that phone call had come about with Josh on the other end and it made her smile involuntarily as she reached for the receiver.

Josh watched the smiling face of his soon to be a bride turn from teasing elation to white as a sheet in a matter of seconds. "What is it...Sal?" He was standing behind her and then she passed the phone over to him.

"He has her and now he wants to talk to you, Josh."

THE PAST BITES

CHAPTER 19

It had been 2 hours since they had gotten the phone call from Lucas and neither one of them wanted to admit that they really didn't have a choice. If they wanted to save their friend Anne, it meant that they were going to have to abide by the terms of the agreement put forth by Lucas and his demented and scarred soul.

"I know we have to do this, Josh, but it will be walking into the lion's den or the wolf's lair as the case may be. We both know it's a trap and that him calling you and me out is his way of getting us into one place altogether. I know that you're going to suggest that I stay behind, but there's no way that I'm going to allow you to do this on your own." Sal had this innate need to save both her child and Josh by whatever means necessary. She wasn't even considering her own safety, as motherhood had brought out a new side of her.

She felt strong and independent and she was going to have to use that same strength in order to see this through to the end. "It would be best that you stay behind, but he would know that and probably have some kind contingency plan in place. Besides, I would rather know that you're safe beside me than somewhere that I don't know what's going on. Sal, this really isn't your fight and I can't ask you to stand beside me, although I know that is entirely your decision and not mine to make." Josh knew that Sal would never leave Anne behind, because they were like sisters.

"I would never forgive myself if something happened to my best friend and I wasn't able to be there to try to prevent it. I know that you would do your best to protect her, but I think your priorities lie in taking down Lucas. Believe me, I can understand the sentiment, but I would rather get out alive with Anne, than to exact some sort of revenge. I know that you haven't gotten over the fact that he punched me in the stomach like that. He only did that to get a reaction and I think it worked." She watched the man that she loved struggle with what could be a life and death decision. She had no doubt that he would kill for her, but could she really ask him to do something like that.

"If we do this together, then I will ask you to follow my lead implicitly. This is the only way I'm going to allow you to come with me. If I sense that there is danger near, I will try to hide you someplace were they can't find you. Then you will be able to leave me behind and I don't want you to argue with me. You and the baby are the only things that are important." Just like Sal, Josh did not care about his own safety and only cared for the safety of her and the baby. If only they knew that they were thinking the same thing, they might reconsider their position.

"Josh, whatever we do, we're going to have to be prepared for just about anything, as Lucas will not want to hurt you, not until I am captured and you can watch as I die by his hand." Sal watched as Josh pulled out something from a chest that he had hidden underneath the bed. It was written in hieroglyphics and some kind of language that she didn't understand. There was an old and decrepit lock and he produced a key.

"I was hoping that I wouldn't have to resort to these measures, but it appears I'm going to have to turn into something that I had long forgotten about. You see, when I first was turned so many years ago, I began to rampage with no semblance of what life really was. I was the thing that went bump in the night and I was what kids were warned about before they went to sleep at night. I killed without mercy and it wasn't until a few years after I did change that I began to find my humanity again."

"You really don't owe me any explanation and you've already told me more than enough. I'm going to stand by you and for you to think that I could leave you makes me think that you don't really know me at all." Sal felt like Josh was her second half, the piece that was missing from her life and the only reason for her to go on. Without him, she was a barren wasteland, but she would have to pick herself up to care for the child that belonged to the both of them.

"I just want you to know what kind of man I was, but that man has long been dead and buried. I wasn't even that kind of man when I met Lucas. He didn't even know that I was a werewolf and I bumped into him when I went to see my one true love before you. She was old and I had been with her for longer than I can remember, but I never aged and she did. I saw Lucas as my saving grace, somebody that I could help in his moment of need. I was arrogant and foolish and I thought that I was some kind of god that could give him the gift of life through my bite." Josh hadn't said anything about this since the day it happened and he really didn't relish reliving those memories all over again.

Sal saw what he was lifting from the chest and it was so small that she really didn't think that it could do all that much damage. "Josh, I have to commend you on at least taking the risk of helping somebody. It's too bad that it didn't work out the way you planned, but rarely in life anything does. I would think that for your experiences that you would know that by now." She held the thing in her hand, looking at it strangely and then placing it where nobody would know to look.

"That has been in my possession for a very long time and to be honest; I really forgot I had it. It just goes to show that once you find any kind of normal existence, you begin to pretend that you are not the monster underneath the sheep's clothing. I forgot that monster existed and I embraced the legacy of the wolf within me. I actually thought of it as a part of myself, when in reality it is an entirely separate entity altogether." He didn't want to admit it, but there were times that he wished that he wasn't a werewolf.

"This is no time for self recrimination and you have to get past that you did this man wrong. He has to know that you did your best and that is all that anybody can ask of you. I mean, what you did for me could've gone wrong, but it didn't. I will say that I'm still coming to terms with my new physique, but I feel more powerful with the baby within me and I think that it's his power and mine that is being combined into one. I don't even know how to describe this to you, only to say that we are feeding off of each other." Sal felt the baby kick and the little guy was getting bigger as each day passed.

"I still say that there is more of you to love and I don't care if you get another 50 pounds, I will still love you with all my heart." He wasn't sure that she believed him, but he had to do what he could to make her see that life was nothing without her. "We don't have to be to the meeting place until tomorrow afternoon, so until then, I think that he will keep Anne alive, just to make sure that we come as requested."

"Josh, I don't understand why I didn't feel him in the boutique before he announced his presence." That was the one thing that puzzled her, because if he was bitten, then shouldn't they have this sixth sense that the other was around. That didn't seem to be with Lucas, or maybe it had to do with a family connection or something along those lines.

Josh felt like a trapped animal and there was really nothing he could do until tomorrow afternoon. He didn't even give them the location, only saying that he was going to call them and tell them what to do next. If he knew Lucas as well as he thought he did, he would make sure that there were no holes in his plan, at least nothing that he could perceive. It didn't mean that there wasn't an opening, something he could use to fight back, but he wouldn't know that until he saw it for his own eyes.

"That's just it and he's not really a werewolf. I thought that I had bitten him strong enough, but it wasn't nearly enough to give him the same transformation. Over the years, I have perfected it, which is the reason why you didn't have any adverse side effects. With him, he was my first and you could say that I was working without a net. I didn't even want to do it, but his persistence was almost as powerful and determined as you were." He was walking back and forth, still looking at his bride to be and wondering why the hell she had even gotten involved with him in the first place.

"He's not a werewolf...so what does that make him?"

"I really don't know how to answer that and I've been trying to find that answer all across the globe. There doesn't seem to be a real name for what he is and I have begun to give him the moniker of Wolfan...a crossbreed of human and werewolf. Once I saw that he was not changing as necessary, I began to see that

I was wrong and that my arrogance had played a big part in me trying to cure something that was incurable. Apparently, there are diseases that a werewolf's bite will not cure and the one that was ravaging his organs was one of those."

"This Wolfan, as you put it, still has this disease and I'm beginning to see that the ravages of time have not been kind to Lucas."

"Sal, he had this zest for life that I found addictive and I didn't see any reason why that extra little something had to be extinguished. Again, I was foolish, but I was young." Josh seized Sal at the waist and pulled her towards him, until they were falling onto the bed with him on the bottom.

CHAPTER 20

"Josh, I'm not sure if this is appropriate, but I couldn't say no to you even if I wanted to. It has been too long since we've been together and I know that you have been trying to protect me and the baby by not pushing sex on either one of us. I already told you that the Dr. said that it was perfectly normal to have relations, but we have to be careful." Sal had her hands busy at his shirt, opening it up one button at a time, in order to prolong the pleasure of seeing his body being revealed.

As she came down to the last one, she opened it up and peeled away the fabric, allowing his muscles to bulge obscenely. There was one love muscle that she found pushing up against her crotch that had now grown to more than a proportional size. The elongated piece of pipe between his legs was making her remember the first time that they had sex last summer. It was a magical evening and soon they were both letting their passions overwhelm them to the point that they didn't care if anybody heard them scream in ecstasy.

This was a little different, because this was exactly what they needed in order to recharge and get ready for the meeting with Lucas. Her only hope was that Anne was being well taken care of and that she wasn't trying to be a hero. They'd known each other for a long time and Sal knew that Anne could be quite the firecracker. She didn't allow anybody to stand up to her and if they tried, she would knock them down with one punch. Having a friend with a short fuse was hard sometimes, but it came in handy others.

"I know that this is not appropriate, but I just couldn't stand not touching you any longer, Sal. I thought that I was making a sacrifice, but now I see that it is only hurting the both of us not to let our passions take us over. We need this and if this is the last time that we are ever together, I want it to be something that we can look back at fondly. Believe me, I don't want you to have to leave me, but I would hope that you would see that it was the best for everybody. If it comes down to your survival, I would hope that you would do what's right for you and the baby." He could feel the heat of her groin against his private area and it was igniting a small spark that was slowly turning into a full blown fire between his legs.

"Let's put all of this ugliness to the back burner for the time being and enjoy a moment of reprieve." She raked her nails over his nipples, hearing him gasp and watching his body arch into the air in response. "Josh, I know that we are close to having this baby and that any day he will arrive. When that happens, we might be able to go back to our regular routine, but I imagine that he is going to be quite the handful." Sal pinched his nipples, bringing her face down until her teeth were touching his neck. She bit into the surface, not too hard to break the skin, but hard enough to make him tremble under her touch.

"I need you in my life, Sal and if I have to sacrifice mine for yours, then I will do that. I know that you'll try to stop me, but believe me once I have something in my head, there's virtually nothing that can change my mind." He was lifting the fabric of the cloth on her body, letting it fall off of her body like a piece of paper. Her nipples drew him to her and she was soon accosted with his tongue going from one nipple to the other. He was pulling them with his teeth, hearing her sigh with contentment and knowing that he was on the right path to her much needed orgasm.

"I need you, Josh and the sooner that you get it through your thick skull that I am not going anywhere, the better off you will be. I have never shied away from a fight and I don't intend to start now. I told you that the baby has given me a new strength and it might be something that we can use to our advantage. We're going to need everything that we have in order to come out of this unscathed. I know that either you or Lucas will not walk away from this, but god help me I hope that it's him that dies at your hand. I don't like saying that, because he has obviously had a bad time of it and is only lashing out because what he thought was going to happen didn't." Sal cupped Josh's head to her chest, while at the same time grinding around on a circle against his most prominent member.

"You're stubborn, sexy, funny, strong, and confident and the list goes on. There are so many adjectives to describe you that it isn't funny. All of this makes you the woman that I fell in love with and I wouldn't ask you to change anything about you. I accept you for all of that, including your faults and everything that makes you who you are." He had his hands on her waist and was moving up and down her side, making her feel these shivers run up and down her spine.

Before she had a chance to react, she was turned so that she was lying on her back with him now peeling away those panties and tossing them to the side. He lifted her legs, found her pussy split wide open and ready to receive his tongue. "Oh god...get in there deep." He didn't need her to guide his actions, because he was already applying his tongue to the center of her moist hole. He felt the amazing heat coming from within and then was subjected to that same heat as his tongue slipped between her folds.

Reaching up, he played with her breasts, twisting her nipples in such a way that it was enhancing the experience for her.

"If there's anything that I can't get used to, it's the wonderful taste that lingers on my tongue every time that I eat this amazing pussy of yours." He punctuated that with his tongue stabbing deep within and then coming back out to move it up her slit and around her clit without actually touching it. He did this several times, feeling her legs jerk and her toes begin to point in opposite directions. Her legs began to rise, until they were resting on his shoulders and soon more beating a drum on his back.

Sal pushed her pelvis up into his face, grabbing onto the back of his head and whitewashing his lips with her juices. "Fuck...fuck...YESSSSSSS." She felt her teeth begin to project and that had never happened when there was no full moon. Hair began to sprout along the back of her hands and then she was turning her head and ripping into the sheets and pillow. She was growling and letting the beast come out, although she didn't seem to have a choice in the matter. If she had to make a guess, she would believe that the kid was playing a huge part in bringing out the beast.

Josh saw her change and pulled his tongue out just long enough to grab onto his package and push it against her lips. Once his cock head was inside her, the rest followed suit with a suctioning sensation that he had never felt before. He felt her wrap her legs around his waist with her arms around his neck and then they were kissing like mad passionate lovers.

"Sal, this is a different side of you, but I think I like it." This time, he felt her shift her weight and before long she was once again riding astride him. Her knees were on either side of his rib cage and she was using her massive and strong thighs to raise and drop her weight onto his midsection. "That hole is so fucking tight...and fucking hot...my god...what are you doing to me?"

Josh could feel this buildup of pressure between his legs and it felt like it was going to burst out of him at any second. She was smiling with her half werewolf transformation and part of her wasn't even there anymore. She moved her hand down until it was situated over her clit and just one touch made her scream like a banshee in heat.

Her orgasm strangled his man missile, launching the rocket and releasing the switch that allowed his cream to spill forth. He bucked underneath her, held her firmly against his waist and unloaded what felt like a month-long abstinence into her body. He felt every single spurt and could feel her muscular insides rippling along his shaft. He was powerless, as she siphoned out every single drop and left him a shell of his former self.

As she was coming down from the afterglow, she could see her reflection in the mirror and saw that her transformation was coming back full circle. Her body was now the same curvaceous frame that she was before without the hair and long canine teeth that had rendered the sheets and pillow case to ribbons. Stuffing was everywhere and she started to laugh maniacally, falling onto the mattress on her side to give the baby as much comfort as she could.

"Sal, I don't think I've ever seen anybody pregnant like that before do something like that. It had to be a first or at least a first as far as I'm concerned.

It appears that you're right and that the baby is causing some undue side effects during the pregnancy. I could feel your knees pressing against my rib cage and I think you almost broke one. It's a good thing that I heal quickly, because walking into this battle with a broken rib wouldn't exactly be conducive to victory." He lay there looking at her, running his hands down over her frame and loving every pound that she had put on during the pregnancy.

He didn't even care that she was at least 50 pounds heavier and had no desire to see her change in any way. If she wanted to stay this way after giving birth, he would certainly give his blessing, but that was a decision left up to her.

"I don't think I've ever felt like that before and I think the baby made the wolf emerge prematurely. It was interesting to feel it happening and we were making love and then we weren't making love at all. We were fucking like wild animals and I felt an orgasm that was by far the biggest that I've had in my life. Everything about that experience makes me want to do it again, so I am just going to put it out there and ask you if you would consider having more kids after this one." She wasn't sure what his answer was going to be, not until he kissed her and then pulled away with a huge smile on his face.

"I've always wanted a big family and when we get through this, I would like to have at least three more. I don't even care if they are boys or girls, because I will love them regardless of their sex and gender. We will have our own pack and if anybody comes up against us, they will realize quickly that we have more bite than bark. In fact, I don't think Lucas has any idea what's coming and to say that he is underestimating us is an understatement." After this experience with Sal's new self, Josh began to contemplate victory instead of defeat. He would do whatever was needed to protect his family, regardless of his own personal relationship with Lucas from the past. If Lucas couldn't leave this alone, then he would have no choice but to fight back in whatever way he could.

"I'm glad to hear that, because I've never actually wanted a huge family, but then you come along. Having you in my life has changed my opinion on a lot of things and I want you to know that your secret of being a werewolf has only made us stronger as a family. We will go in there to this meeting with our head held high and if need be, we will fight as dirty as necessary. Normally, I would think that the honorable thing to do was to fight with honor, but he certainly wasn't acting honorable by taking my friend." Sal had this fire inside her, an ignition of stamina that came about during sex play that she was going to tap into. The kid was their secret weapon but something told her that it wouldn't allow anything to happen to his parents.

"I don't feel that this is a losing battle anymore, Sal. In fact, I think that we can actually win this thing, as long as we keep our heads and keep alert to any other dangers that may present themselves. We also have to contend with Reginald, because we still don't know where his allegiance lies. He obviously found me because of his father, but is he of the same cloth and does the apple fall far from the tree? I guess we won't know that until we see him for ourselves and then we might be able to get a better read on the situation."

Sal was lying there with her hand on his chest, feeling his heart beating fast, but then slowing back down to a manageable level within seconds. "If he wants to fight the family, then we will fight him as a family and together we will end his miserable life. I still don't understand why he just didn't kill himself, because if I was suffering, I would think that I would want to leave this world in my own way."

"I'm sure that he would have done that, but his religion forbids him from ending his own life. Unfortunately, he has to suffer for as long as it takes for the disease to ravage his body and with the semblance of the wolf, he has lived longer than expected. That kind of pain can mess with a man's mind and the only thing that he can think about is revenge." Josh felt sorry for Lucas, but that wasn't going to stop him from ripping him apart when he got the chance. This time, he would not look at him as damaged, but now he was the enemy and he knew exactly what he had to do with his enemies.

They slept in each other's arms, holding each other and enjoying this moment of peace before war. When they awoke to the sound of blue jays outside the window, they smiled at each other, but then that smile faded when they realized that today was the day. He didn't want to admit that his sins had come back to haunt him, but he was going to have to deal with it nonetheless. There was no point in dragging this out and they both got up, with Josh going to have a shower, while Sal went over to her closet to find something suitable to wear.

She wanted something that would be easy to get into, easy to maneuver in and something that would make it easier for her to attack with as much damage as possible.

She put on a pair of jeans and a dark blue sweater over her bountiful bosom. "I know you had reservations about killing him, but I see in your eyes that you don't have that reservation anymore. You won't hesitate when the opportunity presents itself and believe me I won't hesitate either. We have too much to live for to let past grievances get in the way of our happiness. He should know that you've done everything to make this right, including traveling the globe in order to find a cure. You only faked your death because you didn't want him to continue to search in vain. You wanted him to concentrate on getting better or at least conserving his energy long enough to manage the pain." There was a part of Sal that understood how Lucas was thinking and she could only imagine what she would do if she was in his shoes.

Josh came out of the bathroom through the steam with a towel around his waist and holding it with one hand "The only thing that matters is my family and that includes the extended part with Anne. I know that we got off on the wrong foot, but that doesn't mean that I don't want her to be a part of this family. I know that you feel deeply for her and if you feel deeply for her, then I do to."

It must've been her over active hormones, because when he dropped the towel to get dressed, she bit into her knuckle and felt her legs begin to shake uncontrollably. She wanted nothing more than to jump the expanse between them, until she was landing in his arms and taking his hard and unyielding cock between your legs again.

"This kid is going to kill me, Josh. Having him inside me is amping my senses, including my libido, which is right now looking at you like you are a prime steak ready to be devoured. Don't worry, I am going to suppress that part of me for right now, but expect a victory celebration that will leave you panting and satiated. If that doesn't give you incentive to win, then I don't know what will." She smiled, and then they were dressed and walking out of the room.

It wasn't until they got down to the second level, when the phone began to ring again. This time, Josh was the one that answered it. "Josh, it's nice to hear your voice again old friend, but I'm afraid that this is not a cordial phone conversation. There will be a car that will be arriving at your door within 10 minutes and I expect the both of you to be in it. If you are late or one of you decides to stay back, then I will slit Anne's throat from ear to ear. I don't want to do that, but I will if I have to. You know me, Josh and you know that I never go back against my word. If I say that I'm going to do something, then you can take it to the bank that it's going to happen."

"Lucas, this is between us and I am going to give you one last chance to back out. This will be your only chance and once I hang up this phone, then we are no longer friends and we are now enemies. Think about this very hard, because you know what I do to my enemies and you have seen firsthand the wolf at work. It doesn't matter if I can't change until later tonight, because that wolf is still in me and gives me more than I can ever ask for. I don't want to do this and I would rather we go our separate ways and never see each other again."

"I really don't care what you want, Josh and the decision is out of your hands. Be ready and come unarmed, because you will be searched from head to toe when you arrive. There will also be a metal detector to determine if you are hiding anything on your person. If you want to do the honorable thing, I would suggest that you kill yourself now. If you do this, I will leave your family alone and they can live with the pain and loss. Unfortunately, I know that you are selfish and that you would never take me up on that offer."

"If I thought that you were serious and that you would abide by your word, I might consider it. As it is, I really don't believe anything you have to say anymore, Lucas, especially after you punched my wife to be in the stomach. I thought that you had more sense than that, but you have only enraged me to the point that I have to do this for my family. I'm not going to kill myself, but you can rest assured that my hands will find its way around your throat."

"Josh, that's the animal that I want to see and it wouldn't be a fair fight without the both of us being at our best. I'll see you soon my old friend and now current enemy. I'm going to take great pleasure in killing your lover and your kid and then I will hand you the knife and let you finish it once and for all. If you don't have the guts to plunge it into your own chest, then I will be more than happy to do it for you." With that, the line went dead and Josh leaned in with his forehead against the wall.

"I gave him an out and he didn't take it, so this is going to happen whether we want it to or not." They only had 10 minutes, so they stood side by side at the door with Sal leaning her head on his shoulder and him looking towards the future. "We're going to have to be prepared for anything, because he doesn't like to lose. Any time that he was close to losing, he would cheat. He's not above anything, but be aware that he likes to play tricks." He remembered many times that they had fought together, but that ended when he started to show signs of that degenerative disease was returning.

Josh had to listen to him beg to try it again, but he couldn't do that because it was a one time thing. It wasn't like he could bite him again and start the process all over again. Once the bite had taken, whatever happened from then was going to happen regardless of how they felt about it. It became a source of contention between them and it became painfully obvious that Josh couldn't stay there and listen to him whine and complain any longer. Josh knew that he should've stayed and tried to convince him that there was nothing that he could do, but Lucas wasn't listening. He was constantly trying to push his buttons, make him tear him apart and he was almost successful.

"Josh, I would say that we could run away, but I get this feeling that his reach is longer than his arms and then there's Anne to worry about. We would just be postponing the inevitable, but at least it would give us a chance to have the baby first. That way we could make sure that it was safe and we could make sure that somebody that we trust was raising it. I really don't know how we would be able to do that, because I don't know any werewolf's and I doubt that you follow in some kind of circle."

"There's no point with any of this and I've already decided that this is going to happen." Josh had this urge to take her by the hand and rush to the Airport, fly off to parts unknown and try to keep one step ahead of Lucas. It wouldn't work, but maybe it would give them time to be a family before he came calling with his revenge. Once again, he knew that it was only a matter of time and it's not like Lucas not to have some kind of plan in mind in case they were to chicken out.

They looked out the window and saw two black sedans on either side of the road with men with automatic weapons at the ready. They were waiting for them to make a break for it and then they were going to gun them down in cold blood in the middle of the street. There was even one with a video camera, most likely to send the signal back to Lucas in real time, so that he wouldn't miss the gory details of their demise.

CHAPTER 21

"Sal, I don't think we're going to have a choice in the matter. It appears that Lucas has some company waiting for us." They were both contemplating what to do, but knowing full well that they really couldn't leave Anne in the clutches of a madman. They were going to have to follow his directions to the letter, which included walking out of this house and over to a nearby car that had just pulled up to the curb.

They walked towards the car, when the driver got out and met them halfway with a letter. "The person that hired me to take you to the Airport wants you to read this letter. Please don't tell me anything that is going on, because I really don't want to know. The only thing I'm concerned with is getting my money and getting the hell away from him as soon as possible. Just between us, I am a little afraid of him and I've only heard him on the phone. I don't know exactly what you've got yourself into, but I have a family and I don't want any part of it." He opened the door, allowing them to enter and then slammed the door behind them with the click of the lock following.

Sal tore into the letter and Josh was right there reading over her shoulder "Josh, in my heart, I know that you did everything you could, but that doesn't negate the fact that I am dying. I wish that I had the guts to kill myself, but my religious beliefs forbid me from doing that. There are times that I hope that you would come back and finish me off yourself, but you never did. I suppose over the years I've become jaded and with the drugs I'm on, I'm sure that I've gone a little bit crazy. Anyway, I think that I've gotten off subject and this car is going to drive you to the airport where a chartered jet is waiting for you fueled and ready to go. You are to get onto it without any questions and you're not to speak to anyone, unless you are spoken to first. If you can't do this, I will kill Anne, cut her up in little pieces and send her back to you one piece at a time."

"Sal, I'm sorry that I had to get you and your friend into this, because this is a fight that should be between him and me. He was usually an honorable man, but I can see that the drugs that he is on and the time that has elapsed have corrupted his mind." Josh could still remember the last day that he had spent with Lucas, holding him and listening to him moan in pain through the night. The next five hours was excruciating, but he couldn't bring himself to tear himself away from him. He was a coward for leaving him like that in the morning and it was the most painful decision that he had ever made.

"Josh, like I've said before, this is a family problem to deal with now. You can't beat yourself up forever and you're going to have to put it aside in order to keep your mind clear. I think he is only using this letter to confuse you, make you think about past indiscretions and leave you open for attack. This is his way of stopping you from having your A game. There was one student of mine that enjoyed manipulation and it wasn't until you called him on it that he would back down." Sal was trying to keep his mind on what needed to be done and get his mind out of the past where it was going to be of no use to anybody.

"Don't you think that I've tried to put it in the past, but he insists on bringing it back around. I know that I did him wrong, but I was hoping that I would never hear from him again. That's the reason why I faked my death, changed my last name and went far away. I'm still surprised that he was able to find me, but I don't think he was working alone. I think that is son has designs on his empire and that he was more than happy to track me down. He wants us to fight to the death and he's hoping that his father will be a casualty. He doesn't care about me and the only thing he cares about is money." Josh had done his own research and found out that Lucas' son was planning a hostile takeover.

"I should've known that he had his own agenda, but I really thought that he was just being a good son. If you're right, Josh, then he'll want to do that right away, while his father's attention is distracted to us. We could interfere and tell his father what he is planning, but I think that him losing his throne might be exactly what we need to turn the tables. If we can get out of this in one piece, then he won't have the resources to track us down again. Once the power is in his son's hand, then I don't think even Lucas will be able to persuade his son to help him anymore."

"You would have made a great warrior back in the day, Sal and you really do think outside the box. That is a trait that is rare and most people see things in black and white, when there are obviously shades of gray. I think that you were born in the wrong era and that you and I could've been a formidable werewolf couple in the past. There would have been nobody that could stand up to us. With this newborn we would be an unstoppable pack." Josh had watched her grow and the baby was due any time now, but hopefully he would hold off until they were able to finish this nasty business.

Sal grabbed Josh's hand, placed it on her stomach so that she could see his reaction as the kid pounded a drum against her belly. "I don't know how he knows, but I think this kid has an idea of what we're going up against. Even in the fetus, he wants to come out and fight alongside us. I have to say that we have a little fighter on our hands and I do hope that doesn't translate into being a bully in school. We're going to have to teach him to keep his temper in check." She had seen her fair share of bullies in school and she knew that they were only bullies because they were damaged as children.

Almost all of them could be made into productive members of society, but it would come with a price. They would need to go into therapy for at least a year in order to get a handle on why they were pushing people around in the first place.

"I was a bit of a rebel myself when I was a child, but then again I wasn't bitten until I was in my twenties. I don't really know what this kid has in store for it, but we will be there with love to guide and protect him for as long as he needs it. There will be a time that he will want to go out on his own and as parents we are going to have to know when he is ready for the real world. I can show him everything he needs to know about being a werewolf and it will become second nature to him."

"I'm glad that he has a father to guide him, but as a werewolf mother, I can also instill in him the virtues of what is the difference between right and wrong. I don't want him to think that his problems can be solved by his fists. I know how hypocritical that sounds, coming from the both of us going into battle, but I can't help the way I feel." Sal looked out the window and watched the scenery go by, hearing the traffic horns and watching people as they went about their daily lives. None of them had any idea what was behind the curtain and were quite content in believing everything the proverbial wizard was telling them.

If they were to take a moment and look beyond their own eyes, they might see the world as she saw it now. Anne no doubt was finally coming to terms with the fact that there are werewolves. Then again, she might think that she was some kind of pawn in a deadly game between two adversaries that didn't know when to give up.

"As a mother, you'll always be kept on your toes and have to be the one that says no. I will try to be a disciplinarian, but I don't think I'm going to have it in me to look into his eyes and not give in. The bond between father and son is very strong, especially when it comes to werewolves and there's going to come a time when he won't want to listen to either one of us. That is when we're going to have to take a strong stance; at least until we know that he is prepared for what is out there."

"I know how I was when I was a child, Josh and I think this baby is going to be more than just precocious. I think that he is going to be curious about everything and won't know when to quit."

"We can't worry about that right now, Sal because that is for another day. Right now, we have to be ready for whatever Lucas throws at us and believe me he's capable of some heinous acts. I won't go into detail, but we did run in the same pack, at least until he started to degenerate. I can only imagine what kind of pain he goes through on the full moon. It's not like he would have the strength to hunt and he would be a virtual prisoner of his own body. I don't even want to think about what that would do to you mentally and physically for that matter. I do sympathize for what he's been through, but I can't allow him to come after my family in this way."

"I know that he holds a dear spot in your heart, Josh, but you're right and he has gone too far. Had he come up against you on his own, ready to fight, then that might be another matter altogether. I could see the merit in a one on one confrontation, but as you've said, his strength is waning and he probably doesn't think that he could fight fair even if he wanted to. I would say that he has an evil plot in mind and I cringe at thinking what kind of devious plan he has come up with." Sal felt a little antsy, wondering when the other shoe was going to drop, because it was obvious that Lucas wanted them to suffer first.

Always wondering about what they were going to do was causing them to shift nervously in their seat, always on full alert and watching the Damocles sword swing back and forth over their head. The tension was heavy in the air and you could cut it with a knife.

The baby was restless and had no desire to sleep, when his parents were obviously amped up for something.

The car drove straight through the gate of the airport, until it was sitting a idling by the plane that was already gearing up to go. The engine was loud as they were escorted out of the car, where another man with darker complexion, a dark suit and steel cold eyes motioned for them to come closer.

They could feel that their heart was beating and part of them thought that this man was going to kill them and leave their bodies for dead. "You're to be my guest on my island and Lucas will be there. He wants you to know that this is personal, which is the reason why he has come up with this elaborate scheme. He had paid me to keep an eye on you and nothing more, so you don't have to worry that I am going to slit your throat on board. I will however subdue you if you try to run, but I've learned that he has a good friend of yours and that prevents you from trying to leave. I'm what you would call a precaution in case you decide that your friend isn't worth this effort. You will be reunited with her and there is a video conference call on board as proof of life."

Josh wanted to reach out and pummel this man for his part in all of this, but he pulled back and refrained from any kind of violence. "Your mother must be very proud of you and the direction you took in your life. You must know that he is going to try to kill us and yet you still go along with it because of the almighty dollar."

"Josh, I do enjoy my money and my mother has been dead for the past 25 years. If you think that you are going to play on my sympathy, then you are barking up the wrong tree. I have no allegiance to anybody and the only thing I believe in is what I can put into my bank account. If you could match his offer of 25,000,000, then I would certainly entertain the idea of working for you, but I doubt that you have that kind of cash lying around."

"Josh is right and you have no honor." Sal needed to say something, but it was of no use.

"Young lady, it's not a good idea to poke the bear or you might find out that my claws are very sharp." Sal could see that he was serious and that he wasn't kidding or putting on any airs for their benefit. He was here to do a job and nothing more and nothing was going to stop him from collecting his bounty. "This is nothing but business."

A mercenary for hire was somebody that did it for the money, which meant trying to convince him otherwise was pointless. "I guess I have nothing else to say." Sal touched Josh's hand and he held her close, as they walked up the stairs, making of this god awful clanging sound all the way up. They knew that that man was behind them the entire way, but with Anne being a hostage, there was nothing that they could do but follow along like lambs to the slaughter.

When they got on board, they were met with the image of Anne onscreen with Lucas behind her with a knife near her throat. "Josh, I do believe this will suffice for proof of life. If you do exactly what you're told, then maybe she will live. Unfortunately, I can't say the same for you or your new family. I so wanted to kill her and the baby in that boutique, but I knew that it would be more delicious to see you watch them die. My new friend has given me free reign of the island and when you get here, I think you'll see that things are not going to go your way."

"Lucas, why you insist on bringing my family and Anne into this is beyond me. The only reason I can come up with is because you are a weak and you don't think that you can handle me without lording something over my head. The disease must be debilitating and I'm sure that you are having a hard time walking. That would explain the cane and how you have aged over the years. I will make you this promise and I will kill you, even if we were friends at one time. If you think that our past relationship is going to stop me, then you're going to find out in a hurry that you are mistaken." Josh knew that the only way to get to Lucas was to anger him, so that hopefully he would make a mistake that would cost him dearly.

The one thing Josh knew was how to press his buttons and with the illness ravaging his body every second of the day, it was a wonder that he was able to get up in the morning. His mind was not sharp and he was constantly battling headaches. He could even see that that was the case right now, as he was holding his forehead with his hand and pretending that he was just wiping off the sweat.

"I may not be able to fight you fairly, but that doesn't mean that I'm not going to get my revenge for what you've done. I do hope that you enjoy the flight and please have anything you want, as the cupboards are full of caviar and other assorted goodies. You could say this is your last meal and that I am giving the condemned man one last chance to savor some culinary delights." Lucas was so looking forward to them arriving that he had also left a present for them on board.

The screen went black and Sal and Josh looked at each other, while at the same time holding hands, as if they could draw from each other's power and be at one during this time.

"Lucas has requested that you wear something special for the occasion." They thought for sure that it was formal wear and that they were going to die in some kind of ballroom setting. Unfortunately, what this man presented them was nothing short of diabolical. "I don't know what you did to make him angry, but whatever it was must've been serious." He pulled out two collars, not unlike what a dog would wear for their master. "These are going to be affixed to your necks and they are equipped with a sensor that cannot be altered. It will essentially give him a location of where you're at on the island at all times."

"I'm getting a bad feeling about this." Josh already had a suspicion of what was going on in Lucas' mind and the collars had only confirmed what he was thinking.

"He is going to wait until the full moon...and then he is going to hunt you like the animals that you are."

CHAPTER 22

Sal and Josh knew that their time was limited, so they were going to take advantage of their host. Instead of lying back and worrying about something that they shouldn't worry about, they drank champagne and basically had a wonderful time during the flight.

"I don't know how you can relax at a time like this, but I guess if I was in your shoes, I would hopefully do the same thing." They still didn't know his name and he wasn't making any effort to tell them what it was. It was probably better that way, because he didn't want to humanize them. This way he could remain impartial, do what he was required to do and then wash his hands of the entire ordeal. "Both of you should be afraid for your lives, but yet you stand here or more precisely sit here and enjoy the amenities that have been presented to you."

"It's like you've said and we already know what is waiting for us when the plane lands, so we may as well just enjoy the ride and take our minds off of it for the time being. Sal is pregnant and she needs to remain as calm as possible. As for me, I am putting up a strong front in order to protect my family from any adverse effects of stress on the fetus."

"Josh, I wouldn't think that was a fetus and I think it goes without saying that your kid is going to be born very shortly. From what I've heard, you haven't been pregnant for long, which makes me very curious on how a baby such as yours would develop so quickly. If I had the time, I might pursue this course of action, but as it is, you won't be alive long enough to enjoy motherhood or fatherhood. I may not agree with Lucas, but he does pay well and we have been friends for a very long time. Then again, I'm not sure if anybody could really be his friend, not with everything that he has gone through."

"So, he told you everything about his illness and what I did to try to help him? You would think that he would be grateful that I tried, but he can't see past his own eyes. He was my friend and I can say that with a straight face and mean it. He was a good man at one time, a fighter, someone that wouldn't back down to anybody. That was the one thing I liked about him and when I turned him that first time, we became more than just blood brothers. We were a family, something that we both were missing in our lives and we found it within each other. He insists on avenging something that wasn't in my control at the time and changing a human to a werewolf was new for me." Josh was trying to make this man see that the Lucas that he knew was somebody else entirely a long time ago.

"I know it was your first time changing a human, but that doesn't take away everything he has gone through since. You abandoned him, left him when he was at his most vulnerable and then his world was turned upside down when he found out that he had a kid of his own. The mother died and Reginald tracked him down and made him become something that he wasn't…a father." Josh could see that this man felt deeply about this, even though he was just doing this primarily for the money.

"I can't apologize more than I've already done and if he wants to go down this road, then he's going to find out that I have teeth. There's no way than I'm just going to lie down and take what he is going to dish out and I never thought that he was a stupid man until now." Josh could see that Sal was keeping out of this and doing everything in her power to keep the kid from announcing himself too early. "This has gone too far as it is and the moment that he put his hands on my child and the mother of said child was the final straw. He should've known that I wouldn't back down, but I was going to give him an out, until he took our friend Anne."

Even though they were going into certain battle, didn't mean that Sal couldn't admire the fact that her one true love had included her best friend into the family. Ever since Anne was kidnapped, Sal could see that Josh was taking this personally. It wasn't just about her and the child, but Anne was important to her, so she was important to Josh as well.

"I understand that you've apologized and I understand that you were young, but actions have consequences. It might've been a better fate that you left him to die on his own accord, but with the bite, you allowed his disease to stay with him for triple the time. The fact that he changes somewhat on the full moon is debilitating and he can't even do the one thing that werewolf's do on the full moon...hunt. I think that's the reason why he has decided to take you to my island."

"I know what he's doing and the one thing he knows about me is that I never run away. For him to have those people outside our house in case we did run, only confirms to me that he isn't the same man that I knew before. He's been poisoned, not just in his body, but also in his mind. That makes him dangerous, unpredictable and I think that is going to be his downfall. I know that you are only doing this for the money and if you were doing it for him, it might make me angry enough to kill you after I'm done with him. As it is, I can understand monetary concerns, so I'm going to give you a free pass."

"That's so nice of you, Josh and whatever will I do to repay you for this kindness? If you didn't notice, I was being sarcastic and I really don't care for you. He will kill you and your entire family and there will be absolutely nothing you can do about it."

"Never let it be said that I didn't give you fair warning. This was a fight that should've been left to me and him, but he has involved my entire family and for that there can be no forgiveness. Trust me, when I say that I am more than capable of dealing with him and if I have to deal with you, then so be it." Josh picked up his glass of champagne, smiling evilly at this man, making him back away one step. It was enough to know that he had gotten through to him on some level, but it wasn't nearly enough to stop him from bringing them to Lucas. "It might be good to know that his son is about to take over his empire and where will your money be when that happens?"

"That's a lie and even though Reginald doesn't see everything from Lucas' point of view, doesn't mean that he's going to betray him. You're just saying this to confuse me, but all you've done is make me see you as annoying. Reginald would never go against his own father."

"Believe what you want, I just thought that you should have fair warning. I didn't even have to give you that kind of respect, but I thought it was in your best interest to know the facts going in. After all, you say that this is only about the money. Take that away and then what do you have?"

"I don't want to hear this and I know that you're just trying to get underneath my skin. It's not going to work." In fact, it was working quite well and now this man was thinking about what Josh had to say. If daddy was on his way out, then the son certainly wouldn't have any love lost for him. They didn't even know each other and had never seen each other face to face.

"I know you don't want to hear this, but it is the truth and there is an easy way to confirm this. All you have to do is contact somebody on the board and I'm sure that somebody like you has those kinds of resources. If you do that, I'm afraid you're going to find out the awful truth that Lucas doesn't have a pot to piss in. I'm sure that Reginald will keep his father well maintained, but any other extravagant expenses like paying you would be out of the question." Josh could see in the man's eyes that he was contemplating what he was saying and it wasn't going to be long before he made a mad dash to make contact with one of those board members.

"I have work to do, so enjoy your freedom for as long as it lasts, because it's going to be over before you know it. Lucas will kill the both of you and I will be left with millions of dollars in my account. He has always been a man of his word and I don't think that's going to change this time."

Sal watched the whole thing and knew that Josh was only trying to undermine his relationship with Lucas. If they were going to turn him into a traitor, then they would need every bit of information at their disposal. "I hope you know what you're doing, Josh, because you are playing a very dangerous game with a man that doesn't care about anything besides money." Sal could feel the baby, but at least it was still and not doing much moving around.

"I know exactly what I'm doing and I've been playing these kinds of mind games for a very long time. I thought that I was through with that type of life, but it appears that it's like riding a bicycle. You never forget what you truly are underneath all of this, even though I've tried on several occasions to walk away, only to be pulled back in again." He felt like a caged animal, his fingers drumming incessantly on the armrest and his eyes constantly darting from one corner of the plane to the other. "This man is going to find out what I told him was the truth and then we'll see where his loyalties lay."

"I understand that you think that you can use the fact that Reginald is making a hostile play for the empire. The only thing I don't understand is why you think that's going to make much of the different to this man. Yes, he obviously enjoys the wealth and fortune that comes from the relationship with Lucas, but it's painfully obvious that there is a little bit more to it than that. He still doesn't like you and the way that you left Lucas to fend for himself, so even without the money, he might just decide to go along with Lucas' plan anyway."

"Sal, I know that it's a risk, but it's a calculated risk. I've been watching this man and I can see that he's visibly concerned about his funds. It's possible that he will work with us on principle alone. I don't think he's used to somebody backing out on a deal and I really don't believe that he's going to take that kindly." Josh was only guessing at this point, but he had a good suspicion that this man would want some kind of retribution for losing a small fortune...namely $25,000,000.

"I just don't think that we should put all our eggs in one basket, especially with Anne still a prisoner."

CHAPTER 23

"I hope you know that I don't understand any of this. You can't really believe that you were bitten by a werewolf. You have to be crazy to believe any such nonsense." Anne was tied up to a chair, the ropes digging into her skin and leaving behind red welts that would probably take days to heal. Even though she was in considerable discomfort, didn't mean that she was going to sit there and do nothing. "Werewolves don't exist and for you to think otherwise only makes you look demented. Maybe you and Josh should form some kind of club."

"I'm beginning to think that it wasn't such a good idea to take you for a hostage. You really do talk too much and if you don't be quiet, then I'm going to have to do something to make you shut up. I was hoping that I wouldn't have to resort to those measures, but you are seriously getting on my last nerve. Why you don't see what's right in your face is beyond me, but your belief in werewolves is beside the point. It really doesn't matter if you believe or not, because you are just a pawn in a chess game that is going to be won by me. If I have to sacrifice you in the course of the game, then I have no problem slitting your throat and making my point crystal clear."

"I know that your name is Lucas and that you have this insane idea that Josh tried to cure you. That has to be the craziest thing that I've ever heard and I've heard some real stories in my day."

"Young lady, if you don't believe in werewolves, then you're going to believe before this night is over. These cameras in front of you record practically the entire island in one form or another. It will give us a blow by blow of their transformation and then you are going to watch as I pick up this loaded rifle and walk out of this room with the express purpose of killing him and his family. Once you see it for yourself, there will be no going back and that might be just the punishment that is required for your services. I might just want you to live with the knowledge that your friend was telling you the truth and that you decided to close your eyes."

"I didn't close my eyes and I did some research and found photographs that went back many years. Reginald came to me, telling me that I should back down, but I thought that he was foolish. Again, I can't explain the photographs, except to say that it must be a family member, because it can't be Josh in those pictures. It would make him an old man and if he is an old man, then he is on a new drug that should be made public."

"I don't know why you don't see it, but it's going to be fascinating when you finally come to terms with all of this. Anne, I was right where you're at 80 years ago, but I decided to keep an open mind, because I needed the quick fix. You can imagine my surprise when a friend of mine decided to come clean and tell me that he was a werewolf. I thought that he was crazy too, but then the full moon changed all that. It will do the same thing for you." Lucas had taken her because he wanted an edge, something that he could use to persuade both Josh and Sal to come to him on his own terms.

If he didn't have Anne, then Josh would come alone, using his vast knowledge of being a werewolf to his advantage, which was something that he couldn't have. He did however find something all these years hunting for a cure to his illness. In the Congo, he had come across an old village that knew about werewolves. They found an enzyme in a tree bark that keeps the wolf from coming out. The tree in question was very rare and acquiring more than 3 doses was impossible. He was down to his last dose and he was going to make good use of it. By staying mostly human, he would have the satisfaction of hunting Lucas and Sal. That way he could kill them and watch them die. It would be a fitting end to his painful existence and three weeks from today would be his final breath on this planet.

"I don't know how you think you can get away with this, because people will be looking for me when they find that I'm missing. I've only known Josh for a little while, but I can tell you that he won't back down from a fight. I've seen men twice his size cower in front of me when I have them on the spot, but he is different. Let's say for argument's sake that he is a werewolf, then you really think that you have what it takes to destroy the love that they have together.

You don't know anything about mothers and fathers and if you threaten their child, there is virtually nothing that they won't do to protect it."

"Anne you do have a fire in your belly and if this was anytime else, I might find that attractive. As it is, you are a means to an end and you might even survive and go back to the life that you've built for yourself. Unfortunately, you're going to have to leave knowing that you being my hostage was the reason for your friend's death. It kinda gives me a giddy thrill knowing that you will live with that guilt, but maybe that's just the masochist side of me coming out."

"Lucas, I really hope you've thought this through, because one wrong move and he will be all over you like a pit bull. There's still time to back out of this and you can leave the island without anybody having any idea of where you're going. You don't even have to untie me, because they can do that when they get here." She was trying her best to untie the knots that were keeping her bound to the chair but unfortunately it was unlike any knot that she had ever seen before. There was something about it that made it get tighter as she struggled to break free. It was burning into her wrists that she had no doubt that there would be a red welt around her wrist after this was all said and done.

"I have thought this through this is the only thing that has given me meaning for the past few years. He tried to trick me by faking his own death, but I found out. I thought for sure that I had lost my chance, but that hunger for vengeance has always been simmering on the surface. I had nothing to direct it at, until I found out that Josh was alive and well and about to have a family of his own."

"If I have anything to say about it, he will not have anything to do with his child or Sal. Everything that he has done since coming into her life has only hurt her and now he has to answer to me." Anne felt very strongly about her relationship with Sal and she wasn't going to allow any man to stand in between what they had. Josh had stolen her Sal's heart last summer and no matter how hard she tried, Anne just couldn't get her to let him go. "Sal has been hurt enough and it's only a matter time before he leaves in the middle of night like he did the last time. He'll feel guilty for putting his family in jeopardy and then one day, he will finally realize that she is better off without him."

"I think that you're being a bit naïve, Anne and haven't you heard that love conquers all? I know how badly he has wanted a family and for him to get everything that he wants only makes my blood boil even more. I know that this is partly due to the illness, but mostly it has to do with Josh and how he betrayed me. I thought that we were friends and then he gave me false hope. At first everything was fine and I was living inside the inner circle, but then the symptoms started to come back one year after he bit me." Lucas could feel the hatred welling up into a bile that he could taste in his mouth.

"Hey, I've said everything that I'm going to say and now the decision to follow through on this revenge plan is entirely on your shoulders. Just don't come crying to me when you are outwitted. I will give you this and even if you don't survive, I will be always be on his ass to make an honest woman out of my best friend. If he can't do that, then I will show him the door and tell him that he should let it hit him on the way out."

"Normally, I would find your attitude a little hard to take, but it's kind of refreshing to see you stand up for your friend like that. I had that kind of friendship with Josh and I miss it more than you can ever know. I sometimes wish that I could go back, tell him that I didn't want his help and eventually die in his arms like it was supposed to be." Lucas could remember vividly how they had spent that one year carousing and hunting in the woods, seducing young ladies with their animal mystique and just living each day like it was their last. "I think that we could've been friends, you and I, but that ship has already sailed."

"So what exactly are we waiting for now?"

"Anne, I think you can see that the sun is slowly setting and before long the full moon will be at its peak. They should be arriving in the next 20 minutes and then the games can commence." Lucas went to the window, threw open the curtains and looked at the orange ball of the sun as it slowly descended beyond the trees. It was beautiful and it made him feel like he was some kind of god, able to reach out with his bare hands and snatch the sun from where it was now disappearing. "I've waited too long and now that everything is going according to plan, I can finally take him with me to hell."

CHAPTER 24

"I won't be staying with you through this, because this is between the both of you and Lucas. I did look into what you had to say about his son Reginald and it appears that you were correct. Thankfully, I was already paid half up front and I just have to contend with Reginald and make him see that I deserve the rest. If he thinks otherwise, then I'm not above using extreme force to get what I want and I think that you've seen that for yourself. I have a penchant for torture that makes a man blubber like a schoolgirl. I'm sure that we can come to a reasonable arrangement between gentlemen, instead of letting things get out of hand."

Josh had this desire to push his buttons and decided that he didn't have anything to lose "You really don't know Reginald and with his father's money behind him, getting anywhere close to him is going to be a Herculean task. I don't think he trusts his father's judgment anymore and that is the reason why he decided to make this play. If I were him, I would make sure that any of his father's back door dealings were dealt with. He wouldn't want any of that disgusting business to fall on his doorstep."

"Josh, I know what you're trying to do and it's not going to work. I will have my money, even if I have to take it out on Reginald and anybody else that stands in my way. Besides, you needn't worry about me, because either way I am going to find a nice little island with a lot of girls in bikinis and settle down for the long haul. Even 12,500,000 will go a long way. In fact, I would say that that is enough money to live on and not have to worry about working or doing any of this distasteful business ever again. That's not to say that I'm not going to go after Reginald, because it's what was agreed to."

The plane was starting to shift to the right and they could all feel the drop in altitude, as the plane was preparing to land. Outside the window, the island was getting bigger with each second that passed and there was a small airstrip on the far side of the island that was going to be used to bring these two passengers in. "I would say that our business together is about to be concluded and I've already told you that I might come after you for your part in this." Josh was seeing this man smile, folding his arms across his chest and looking at him like he was an ant to be burned alive on a hill.

"You do what you need to do, Josh, knowing full well that if I do get wind that you were coming after me, then I would have to take some precautions. I won't go into detail, but suffice to say that I have friends in low places that will keep me informed of your whereabouts. Let's just say, if you even think about coming after me, then I will be more than ready. I have one rifle that only shoots silver bullets and I think that'll be in more than enough to kill the wolf and you in one shot."

The plane hit the pavement and made them all jerk in their seats, but they were already secured tightly with the seatbelts. The sound of the engine powering down was followed by the screeching of the tires as the rubber met the pavement. Before long, they were taxiing down the runway and then coming to a complete stop in front of a small building that looked like it hadn't been used in ages. In front was an Airport sign, but most of the letters were missing and the only thing that you could really see was the A and the T at the end of it.

Josh and Sal were escorted to the front of the plane, where the door was now open and they could feel the humid heat hitting them in the face. The wind was warm and they could see that the sun was almost gone. It wouldn't be long before the moon made an appearance and then they both would change, right along with Lucas. What they didn't know was that Lucas had the ability now to stop the transformation, so that he could be human when the hunt began.

"I guess that this is our stop. It's been interesting getting to know you, but honestly I hope that we never meet again in any circumstance." Sal took this opportunity to smack him across the face, before turning on her heels and going down the metal railing to the pavement below.

"If anybody else had done that, I would've killed them, but your woman has something that I haven't seen in a long time. Instead of being afraid, she sat there with her eyes staring at me the entire time and making me feel like I am exposed. For your sake, I hope that Lucas does what he intends to do. Trust me when I tell you that you don't want anything to do with me on a more personal level than what you've already seen. I'm capable of so much more than just this kind of business and I've been trained in ways that most people would cringe if they found out."

"That's good to know, but frankly I don't think you have a chance against the wolf. Right now it's itching to get out and I can feel it clawing at my insides and making every effort to rip you apart with its teeth." Josh left him there to think about everything, going out of the plane and standing with Sal as the door closed and the plane turned right around and went back down the same runway that it had come in on.

The deafening roar of the engine as it flew into the open sky made both Sal and Josh look at the only means of escape slowly receding into the twilight. "Sal, I want you to know that there isn't anything in this world that we can't vanquish together. As long as we stand as one, then my old friend Lucas will not have a chance."

"That's not the truth, Josh and I have a few surprises up my sleeve that you'll never see coming. I'm coming for you both, but be rest assured that I will leave you to the last, Josh. It is after all what you deserve for what you did to me. I'm going by the Biblical meaning of an eye for an eye. In my mind, you don't deserve to have that newfound family, not when I am going to lose everything. I know about my son's duplicitous behavior, although, I don't see why I should concern myself with any of that. I won't be here for a very much longer anyway and I was already thinking about retiring and leaving everything in his name." They could hear his voice, but they had no idea where he was, only that there seemed to be speakers hidden within the trees.

"I told your friend on the plane that I would be coming after him, but first I will have to deal with you old friend. I'm through beating myself up over what happened to you, because you were going to die anyway and I gave you years of life. In fact, I don't think you would've had your son Reginald if it wasn't for my intervention." Josh was making one last ditch effort to persuade his old friend to look the other way. "If my math isn't wrong, you had your son 40 years after we first met. Without that bite, you would have died from that disease a long time ago and you would never have met the mother of your child. It is unfortunate that she didn't see it clear to tell you about him and he had to track you down on his own when he was old enough to ask questions."

"I will thank you for my son, but that is as far as the gratitude goes. I really didn't get a chance to see him grow up and essentially we have been strangers to each other for the past couple of years. Maybe things would've been different if I had known him from the very beginning of his life, but I didn't." Josh felt his tongue swelling inside his mouth, his eyes growing bigger and hair began to sprout all over his body.

Sal could feel the same thing and her clothes began to rip as the muscular wolf inside her began to form into the beast that she was. They had changed and were now looking at each other wondering when Lucas would come out to play.

"I can see that you've both changed and I imagine right now you are confused by the fact that I can still talk to you. I'm not a wolf and I found a way to suppress that side of myself on a limited basis. I'm coming for you not as the wolf, but as the man that you have condemned to a life of pain. I have everything I need to hunt you, plus if you think that I am weak, then I will tell you that this drug that I have suppressed the wolf with also gives me power. It makes me faster, more agile and all of my senses are alive. It sounds like a wolf, but in reality it is just a man, but I am more man than you could ever be, Josh."

Telepathically, they were still linked and they both told each other that it was time to hide. They moved in unison, like they knew each other's moves by the back of their hand. They were side to side, with the only difference being that a patch of white on Sal's hind quarters. It was the only way that you could tell them apart, as they showed their teeth and began to sniff the air, like they could send something coming over the wind.

There was no denying that they were being watched, but this was something that they couldn't stop, at least not until they were able to take care of those cameras. They both acted, with each one going up a tree and snatching the camera and smashing it to pieces on the ground below. With each one that they found, they did the exact same thing, making sure that when they doubled back that Lucas would have no idea what was going on.

They continued to blind him, until finally the first shot rang out and barely missed Sal by a few inches. It made the wolf jump back in surprise, but then she bared her fangs and looked for a target to attack. The darkness didn't do anything and both Josh and Sal could see exactly where they were going by not only the light of the moon but also by their own enhanced ocular senses. "That was just a warning shot and something to give you an idea of what I have for you. I had her in my cross hairs, Josh and I decided to play with my prey." Lucas was on the ridge, looking down from above with his rifle perched on his shoulder and his eye up to the scope. This was the first time in a long time that he had felt alive and without the wolf and the disease constantly dragging him down into a pit of pain and suffering, he was now able to concentrate with a little bit of effort on his part.

Josh allayed a message to his bride to be that he was going to try to circle around and come at him from the other side.

Sal didn't like that he was going to go it alone, so she made a dash for the trees on the other side, so that they were both coming at him from different angles.

Chapter 25

They had been playing cat and mouse for the past four or 5 hours, when they finally had a bead on Lucas. They were both in the perfect position to jump out of the foliage and take him by surprise. They were about to do just that, when both of them stopped short and waited. It was like a sixth sense and they both felt that there was something wrong.

Josh used his paws to clear the field in front of him, only to come face to face with a bear trap that would've cut him to ribbons if he stepped any closer to where Lucas was now standing quite still.

Sal did the same thing and found exactly the same thing waiting for her. She had almost walked into a trap that would've caused her great agony and most likely make her little boy inside her scream as well. This was the first time that she had seen how far Lucas was willing to go for revenge and it made her wonder if they could survive the night.

"I'm here, so what are you waiting for an engraved invitation?" Lucas heard nothing, no scraping of tree branches or twigs snapping, but something was telling him that they weren't too far away." I know you're there and I couldn't have made a better target for myself even if I wanted to." He was staring into the darkness, using the drug that he had found in the Congo to light up his corneas. His cones were enhanced and he could sense the both of them were near, but still too far away to really do anything about.

He heard the growl and found it was a sound that was traveling on the wind from either side of him. This was no coincidence and even though they were a family, they were now working alone towards a common goal.

Lucas had his gun at the ready and fired indiscriminately into the trees on either side of him. He was hoping for a lucky break, but once again was disappointed by no sound of agony coming from either side. He waited, listening intently in the vain attempt to block out every other sound besides the sound of the wolf.

When he saw them, he knew that they had circumvented his trap, but this also left them vulnerable. They were showing their dominance by growling with spittle coming out of their mouth. He had the instinct to run, but that would only cause more harm and besides there was no way that he could outrun them as a human.

He started to back away, putting his hands out in front of him so that they knew that he was terrified of dying on this night. Still walking backwards, he watched as they slowly stalked their prey, until the both of them were now walking as one. They had joined up from either side and were now right in front of him with his gun dangling to the side. Lucas knew that if he tried to raise the weapon that they would be on him in a second, so he instead deployed a distraction.

An explosion went off behind them and both Josh and Sal glance back, momentarily leaving Lucas to make a run for it. The plume of smoke was at exactly the spot where the Airport building was located. They both knew that the explosion was meant to distract them and that the explosion itself was contained within the building. They had no doubt that once they arrived back at the airstrip that the building would be destroyed beyond recognition.

They turned at the sound of heavy breathing and knew that they had given Lucas a small moment of reprieve to regroup. They didn't want him to have enough time to spring something else on them, so they hurried along through the foliage, until they were once again face to face with Lucas. He was breathing heavy, his hands on his knees and he really did look like a beaten man.

Sal took one step forward and Josh suddenly realized that Lucas wasn't sweating. This meant that he was playacting being out of breath and was his way to draw them closer. He pounced on Sal and kicked out with his back feet to keep her away, while at the same time he heard the ground give way and found himself on a freefall.

He tried to gain ground, but the only thing he found was air, as something sharp and pointy drove into his back leg all the way out to the other side. He howled and gave out a roar of pain that made Sal look at Lucas for answers.

Lucas walked with a purpose up to the hole of his own making, until he was looking down at his old friend squirming and bleeding quite profusely from the wound in his leg. "That wasn't meant for you, but I do have to admire that you were willing to throw yourself on the grenade for the ones you love. You really have changed, Josh and in the old days you wouldn't have cared about anybody's safety but your own. It appears that falling in love has given you a purpose in life, not unlike the same purpose that I have for killing you. I'll leave you for the moment, as I'm sure that Sal is going to want to rescue you in some way. I don't know exactly how she is going to go about that, but I really don't care. I can tell that you are in a whole lot of pain and that gives me great pleasure. Unfortunately, it's not enough and your death and the death of your family are imminent."

Sal took a step forward, until she saw the gun glinting in the moonlight.

Lucas was standing there with his gun ready, but for some reason he just couldn't kill her without Josh fully aware of what was going on. This would give him no satisfaction and he was just going to have to wait for a better time. He kept the gun trained on his target, watching as her eyes were glowing a yellow rage that couldn't be contained. Lucas wanted the revenge that he had set out to get and he wasn't going to settle for anything less. He took aim and fired one more shot, scraping the hindquarters of Sal. It ripped into the white piece of fur and left behind a distinct red mark. It didn't bleed all that much, but it was more than enough to give Lucas enough time to disappear within the trees.

Sal had a decision to make, whether to go after Lucas and finish this once and for all or help her beloved. Not knowing what to do, she instead followed her heart and looked down to see that Josh was now struggling to remove the long wooden spike that was drove into his leg from the fall. There was really no way for her to go down there, as there were several more spikes that would most likely take her captive as well.

Looking around, she saw a downed tree and went over and used her werewolf strength to tear a large long branch off of that tree. It took a lot of energy for her to drag it over to the hole, drop it down to where Josh was still trying in vain to break free. It landed in such a way that it was now in front of Josh and the other part was sticking up above the hole. If he was going to make a move, this would be the time to do it.

Josh, seeing his freedom at hand, gave a howl of pain, while at the same time pulling that spike out of his leg. It almost made him pass out, but he then shook his head, clearing the cobwebs, before limping lazily over to the branch. He looked up to see Sal with this worried expression on her face and he slowly climbed the branch one paw at a time. It felt like forever, but only took a few minutes before he was lying prone on the ground as Sal as the werewolf was licking his wound. Before long, the healing effects of her tongue were more than enough to stop the flow of blood. It didn't however close the wound, but it did clot it, so that it wouldn't become infected.

It was then that the clouds above them began to circulate, until finally a rain started to fall on top of them. They both looked at each other, knowing that this would slow down Lucas enough for them to elude capture.

CHAPTER 26

The storm continued all through the night and there was one moment there that they were hidden from view within some mud that they saw Lucas walk by scowling and obviously distressed that he couldn't find them. Ironically, had he had his werewolf out to hunt for them, he most likely would have found them in short order. As if was, they were able to keep one step ahead of him by doubling back to those parts in the woods where they had destroyed the cameras.

Sal did everything she could to protect Josh, keeping him warm with her fur and body pressed up against him through the night. She could feel that he was shivering and it wasn't because he was cold, but because of the blood that he had lost. Had she not acted when she did, he most likely would have died there in the pit and that was something that she just couldn't allow. If she could, she would trade places with him in a second, so that she didn't have to not see the pain in his face. His werewolf eyes were dimmed slightly, showing that his energy had been stripped away.

Josh could feel that he was not going to be able to fight against Lucas, but he didn't have the heart to tell Sal that they were going to lose eventually. He tried to keep a brave face, but he sensed that she could see through his false bravado. If he had to, he would sacrifice himself, so that Sal and the baby would have a better chance of surviving. This would give them the opportunity to find Anne and get them all out of here. He knew that this was wishful thinking, because even if he did sacrifice himself, Lucas would not stop until the entire pack had been decimated.

The rain was slowing down, but they could also see that the moon was slowly receding and being replaced by the sunrise. They both felt the change, began writhing on the ground, making these god awful noises that sounded like two animals being torn apart.

Their bodies began to form back to their original human form and before long they were both naked. "Sal, I want you to leave me here and let me take care of Lucas in my own way. Your priorities lie with the baby and your best friend and I can certainly take care of Lucas. I know him and I know how he thinks, so having you out of the line of fire is going to make it easier for me to play his mind games." His leg was in no shape, but he tried and succeeded in getting onto his feet and making it look like he wasn't as hurt as he appeared.

"That's not going to happen; Josh and we're going to get out of here together or not at all." Sal was not stupid and knew that he was hurt worse than he was letting on and was only doing this to make sure that she was safe. It was a man thing to do and a small part of her wanted to commend him on being a good father and provider, but the bigger part of her want to put him in his place. "You don't have to be this way with me and I know that you are in horrible pain." Sal could see that Josh was limping and it looked like he was going to buckle underneath his own weight any second.

"Now this is a picture that is worth 1000 words." Lucas stepped forward, after hearing the anguished cries of them transforming back into human form. He followed that sound like a pied piper all the way back to its source. He was now standing in front of them with his gun trained on Sal and about to pull the trigger.

"If our friendship means anything to you at all, Lucas, you won't do this. She didn't do anything to you and this has always been between the two of us. If you want to kill somebody, then kill me and let Sal and the baby live with the loss of me. That would be a punishment that was worse than death."

"Josh, I do treasure our friendship, even if it was short lived, but my path is clear. Your bitch and the little bastard that she is carrying have to die in front of your eyes. It is the way that has been played out in my mind 1000 times since I found out that you were going to be a father. It's the only way that you're going to know even a semblance of what I've gone through over the years with this illness. It gives me no joy to kill a little baby that hasn't even been born yet, but this is how it has to be."

Sal felt something inside her stir, something that was all encompassing and then suddenly she felt this newfound strength. It wasn't there before and she called upon this strength to leap the distance between her and Lucas. Her claw on her right hand had now come out, slapped the gun out of Lucas' hand and sent it spiraling into a nearby tree. It shattered into four big pieces, essentially useless and it wasn't going to be used to exact the revenge that Lucas wanted.

"How the hell...Argggghhhh." He felt the slash across his face, could feel something wet and reached out to touch his face. What he brought back was blood and he stared at the half human and half werewolf Sal.

He tried to grab for his knife, but once again Sal was too quick for him and she now had it in her hand and was stabbing it into his chest. His eyes went wide, his mouth went slack and his tongue was now hanging out of his mouth. "Nobody comes after my family and lives to tell the tale."

Sal felt compassion for the injured man and she grabbed his head with both clawed appendages and twisted until she heard the snap of his neck. It was a cold comfort that he was dead, as she didn't even know that she was going to do that until the last minute. A feeling came over her that if she allowed him to live that he would continue to hunt them. Even if he only had a short time to live, didn't mean that the risk of him catching up to them wasn't real.

She let him go, watching as his body slumped hard to the ground, where there was no discernible heartbeat and his chest wasn't rising and falling with each breath.

"Sal, that was amazing." Josh had come up to her and was now leaning on her shoulder to look past to see his old friend lying lifeless on the ground. "If you can give me a few minutes, I would like to give him a proper burial. I know that I don't owe him anything, but he deserves that respect."

Instead of leaving him alone, Sal fell to the ground and began to dig with her claws and that supernatural side of herself made a nice hole to bury Lucas in. She was tired, her hands covered in dirt and she was on all fours watching as Josh laid Lucas to rest in this makeshift grave.

Josh did the honors of filling it back in, grabbing two branches and tying them together with a vine. He stabbed into the earth as a way to mark his friends passing and to know exactly where he was now laying his head.

When he was finished, he went to Sal, knelt on the ground and lifted her face to his. She was still showing signs of the werewolf. Her claws were now back to human hands, but her face still showed the yellow eyes and the fangs that went with being a werewolf. He kissed her, letting her know that he was there, only to see that she was now raising her head with this intensity that he had only seen once before.

Before he could react, she was on him in a second, driving her pussy down onto his cock and letting out a howl of pleasure that came from deep within their. Her hefty frame pounded relentlessly against his waist, using his body for her own pleasure and not caring about the man at all. "If this is how you get from being pregnant, then we're going to have to have a lot more babies." Josh thought that inserting a bit of levity into the situation would make her laugh, but she only growled and grinded around in a circle in his lap.

This of course was to provide her the stimulation that she needed to reach a climax, as his shaft was rubbing her clit and then she lifted her body and then brought it down so hard that he thought for sure that she was going to break some of his bones. Instead, she began to shake with her eyes were dancing wildly in her head, as her orgasm grabbed him like a dog with a leash, demanded his seed and he had no choice but to give it up.

"OWOOOOOOOOO." She sat there on top of him, her head thrown back and the veins in her neck straining from the aftermath of what they just did. There were still bits of blood on her body from attacking Lucas, but it was the glow of impending motherhood that was causing Josh to look at her in a newfound light. It made him proud to have her part of his pack and soon they would have another bundle of joy to add to it.

EPILOGUE

They did find Anne and she had witnessed everything from where she was tied up to the chair. Sal went into labor, most likely brought about by the amorous activities that they had just performed on each other in the woods. They were able to call for an extraction, paying for a private helicopter to come out to the island to take them back to the mainland for the birth of their baby.

In a darkened room, Reginald sits and clenches his fist, standing up and grabbing the monitor with both hands. He throws it against the wall, his hand shaking, but then it slowly subsides and he straightens himself out and leaves the room knowing that Sal and Josh were the ones that were responsible for his father's demise. At first, he thought that it was what he wanted, but seeing it firsthand was galling. The only thing he could think about was avenging his father, but he would wait for the right time to strike. This was what his father had taught him and this was really the only time that he was going to listen to him.

"Sal and Josh, you haven't seen the last of me and I hope that you are constantly looking over your shoulder. See you soon." He turned off the light, closed his father's study and would never enter into that domain again.

About The Author

Jodie Sloan loves reading and writing romance stories. Her love for romance began when she had started reading romance stories and grown to love them more as she started writing.

Her passion for writing has motivated her to write several book series of her own. Currently, Jodie Sloan is in the process of writing several more book series that she hopes will be worth reading.

She cherishes her family and takes each day as an opportunity to love, read and write.

Jodie loves to hear your feedback, reach her through:

Facebook

https://www.facebook.com/pages/JodieSloan/180879798753822

Get Future New Releases In This Series For 99 Cents

http://eepurl.com/7jbHr

Check Out My Other Books

Wolf In Disguise: Once Bitten

http://www.amazon.com/dp/B00PH8QGTO

Wolf In Disguise: Never Forgotten

http://www.amazon.com/dp/B00PHJSF5Q

Wolf In Disguise: The Past Bites

http://www.amazon.com/dp/B00PHJSF10

Forbidden Passion

http://www.amazon.com/dp/B00PHF6YQM

Second Chance

http://www.amazon.com/dp/B00PHQ6HO0

Closure

http://www.amazon.com/dp/B00PHF6XZY

Printed in Great Britain
by Amazon